He sat down next to her and she moved slightly, her head coming to rest on his shoulder. He breathed in deeply, getting his fill of her intoxicating scent.

Instinctively he caressed her cheek. Charlotte moved against him, filling him with contented warmth. The crickets started to sing, and for the first time in months a sense of peace entered him, slowly unwinding, spreading out in coils of relaxed ease.

Non! This was insane.

Urgency ripped through him. He needed to be anywhere but on this swing with this woman. He had to leave. Now.

He moved his arm away, the heat of her skin no longer soothing against his, but burning.

Scooping up his paperwork and laptop, he strode down the veranda towards his car. Each step taking him away from the lovely, but absolutely-not-what-he-was-looking-for Charlotte Buchanan. He put one foot in front of the other, refusing to look back.

But, God help him, he wanted to.

Dear Reader

The original idea for this story hit me back in 1995, when I was pegging out nappies for my firstborn. It was special because it was *the* first book I ever wrote. I loved the idea of an independent midwife who balanced her time between community midwifery and hospital midwifery. I loved Xavier and Charlie. But the story wasn't quite good enough, so I put it aside, waiting until I had the skills to tell their story.

I'm thrilled to say that time has arrived. When I peeked into the lives of Xavier and Charlie I asked them this question: What if everything you ever believed in suddenly changed?

Xavier, my deliciously gorgeous French doctor, with an accent that makes your knees go weak, has just realised the woman he thought he would spend his life with has been using him to gain a career advantage. He's packed his bags and come to Australia to restart his life, and he is determined to give all career-minded women a wide berth.

Charlie is a passionate midwife who believes that delivering babies and living in Amaroo is all she needs to be happy.

Suddenly, with Xavier's arrival, her independent midwifery programme is under threat.

In a fictitious town in southern Australia, where the whales come each winter and give birth, Xavier and Charlie battle their attraction for each other and eventually learn that there is more to life than work, and yet work is a vital part of their life.

I hope you enjoy their story, and meeting the wonderful people of Amaroo.

Love

Fiona x

THE
FRENCH DOCTOR'S
MIDWIFE BRIDE

BY
FIONA LOWE

MILLS & BOON®

First published in Great Britain 2007
Harlequin Mills & Boon Limited,
Eton House, 18-24 Paradise Road, Richmond, Surrey TW9 1SR

© Fiona Lowe 2007

ISBN-13: 978 0 263 19803 4
ISBN-10:   0 263 19803 0

Set in Times Roman 1(
15-0507-48618

Printed and bound in Great Britain
by Antony Rowe Ltd, Chippenham, Wiltshire

Always an avid reader, **Fiona Lowe** decided to combine her love of romance with her interest in all things medical, so writing Medical Romance™ was an obvious choice! She lives in a seaside town in southern Australia, where she juggles writing, reading, working and raising two gorgeous sons, with the support of her own real-life hero! You can visit Fiona's website at www.fionalowe.com

Recent titles by the same author:

THE SURGEON'S CHOSEN WIFE
HER MIRACLE BABY
THE NURSE'S LONGED-FOR FAMILY
PREGNANT ON ARRIVAL

To Pam, who supports me and my family in so many special ways, and enjoys nothing better than curling up with a great romance. Thank you!

CHAPTER ONE

CHARLIE BUCHANAN, outreach midwife, made it to her next appointment with barely enough time to catch her breath. But this time she wasn't catching a baby.

She sank into the soft leather chair, and immediately regretted it. The cloying tendrils of fatigue took advantage of her the moment she sat still, wrapping themselves tightly around her. Her shoulders ached from changing her flat tyre on the way into town. She'd give anything for hot food, a warm bath and much-needed sleep.

But it would all have to wait.

'Dr Laurent is ready to see you now.' The new chief of medicine's secretary spoke in clipped tones, casting disapproving looks toward Charlie.

She instinctively ran her hands down her skirt to straighten it, as memories of boarding school washed through her. *Charlotte needs to take more care with her appearance.*

Why hadn't she taken a moment to tame her unruly hair into a neat, thick braid instead of frantically rushing to be on time? She resisted the urge to slap her forehead with her palm. Of course the new doctor would be running late!

The new French doctor had arrived in Amaroo a week ago. According to the hospital grapevine, the dust he'd raised didn't look like it would be settling any time soon. The words 'review' and 'budget' had been muttered a lot in corridors and the cafeteria, along with 'economic rationalist' and 'despot'.

She blew out a breath, letting her body relax. Applying logic, none of this should affect her. Her programme was well established with its own approved budget. This meeting wouldn't be any more than a 'get to know you' session.

She opened the familiar door and stepped into the office.

Standing behind a large desk, talking on the telephone but waving her into a chair was, Charlie assumed, Dr Xavier Laurent. All six feet of him, and probably more.

An immaculately cut charcoal suit clung to his body, emphasising broad shoulders and a narrow waist. The open jacket moved as his arm rose and fell, revealing flashes of a vivid crimson and emerald tie lying against a white shirt.

A 3D image of a solid, muscular chest burned into her mind. Horrified at the unexpected mental picture, she moved her gaze up the length of the tie rather than down. Black hair streaked with silver caressed his temples, adding to his aura of model good looks overlaid with natural authority.

His ebony eyes, ringed with thick dark lashes, gazed at her, their look both charming and scrutinising at the same time.

The butterflies in her stomach fluttered faster, her unease going into overdrive on the back of another sensation she didn't care to examine closely.

She forced herself to meet his penetrating gaze. But looking into those eyes was like falling into the great unknown and she quickly glanced away. The very last thing she needed was to be attracted to the new chief. Not a smart move, professionally or personally.

She didn't do relationships. Relationships meant losing yourself. Relationships forced you to be someone you weren't just to make someone else happy, and that never worked. She knew that misery intimately—bitter experience had taught her well. It had taken half her life to work it out but she knew one thing for sure, she was *never* submerging her own happiness again in an attempt at love.

Dr Laurent put a large, lean hand over the mouthpiece of the phone, smiled and mouthed the words, 'I will be with you in a minute,' and returned to his call.

His deep smile carved into his tanned face, an arrowhead of creases framing his mouth of white teeth. The rays from that smile seared her.

Unwanted heat swirled inside her.

It's a courtesy smile, get a grip, you're just tired. She shoved the mental picture of his smile away with some righteous indignation. *Great, glad I rushed to get here on time.*

Breathing out again, she tried to centre herself and push all emotions away, including her uncharacteristic irritation. Phil Carson, the now retired chief, had often kept her waiting in their meetings and she'd always been resigned, not cross. She swallowed a sigh. Sleep deprivation made her grumpy and she really needed a decent night's sleep. Surely the current Amaroo baby boom would slow down soon.

She deliberately glanced around, forcing her gaze away from the tall, dark, handsome and totally unsettling doctor. Surprise jolted her. Gone were the old fishing prints Phil had loved. In their place hung a large original still life—a bowl of yellow pears sitting against a magenta, teal and Pacific blue background, the vivid colours contrasting with the freshly painted ivory walls.

A large photograph caught her eye. Pink, russet and yellow low-rise European-style buildings, their windows defined by wooden shutters, nestled between craggy green-grey mountains and shimmering azure blue water. Wooden fishing boats bobbed on the sea in front of a pretty but narrow beach. It looked like the Côte d'Azur in France.

She'd spent a wonderful month there once, doing a conversation French course in a small village between Nice and Cannes. She'd loved the area but couldn't help comparing the narrow stone lined beaches to the soft, golden sands of Amaroo.

To her left, a French Provincial-style conference table sat solidly, the walnut wood gleaming in the reflected sunlight that poured in through the large windows. In the centre of the table stood a coffee-pot and fine china cups, their lips outlined with a fine gold band.

In front of her, and completely unrecognisable, stood the desk Phil had used. Instead of the clutter of patient histories and piles of random papers, a computer purred, its screen-saver flashing a geometric design.

The room screamed neat. Nothing was out of place. The pile of files next to the computer sat in perfect alignment, precision in every sharp corner of the brightly coloured folders. The top one read, 'Community Midwifery Programme.'

Charlie's project. Her baby. The result of her integral belief in women caring for women in their own environment during pregnancy and labour.

Quelling her agitation with a deep breath, Charlie sat down and crossed her legs. She immediately noticed a splotch of mud on her knee—a legacy from her flat tyre—and hastily re-crossed her legs the other way to hide the mark. Dr Laurent didn't look like mud would ever dare touch him. The butter-flies took flight again, her stomach churning.

How ridiculous! She was twenty-eight years old, not twelve. She was meeting a professional colleague, not Terror

Tompkins, her old boarding-school principal. She sat up straighter.

He smiled as he dropped the handset back into the phone cradle and strode around the desk, both actions swift and decisive. 'I am sorry to have kept you waiting.' The Rs rolled gently on the wave of his French accent. 'A hospital is a series of interruptions, *non*?' He shrugged, the rising and falling motion of his shoulders travelling the length of his body.

'I am Xavier Laurent, and you must be Charlotte Buchanan. I am pleased to meet you.' He extended his hand forward in greeting, his body moving fluidly.

She pushed her hand forward, trying to concentrate on a professional greeting. His large hand immediately engulfed her smaller one, almost a caressing motion, leaving her palm tingling. She hastily withdrew her hand, balling it into a fist to stop the warm feeling racing up her arm.

Focus! First impressions are vital. 'I am, but most people call me Charlie.'

He tilted his head for a moment, as if absorbing this piece of information, his dark eyes never leaving her face. 'Charlotte is a beautiful feminine name and yet you use a man's name?'

She laughed. 'It's an Australian tradition. If the name is long, we shorten it, if it's a short name, we lengthen it. Charlie was a better option than Blue.'

Confusion creased his brow. 'Blue?'

She smiled. 'It's what Australians call a person with red hair. Crazy, isn't it?'

'It's the slang that causes me problems. My time has been spent between two countries and sometimes I am confused in two different languages.' His laughter rumbled around the room, its low timbre warming her.

'But you've spent more in France than Australia?'

'I came first to Australia when I was nineteen. My Sydney uni friends tried to teach me the Aussie accent and I can say, "G'day, mate."' He spoke the two words in the broad, flat Australian accent and grinned. 'But I think my accent is again stronger as I have been working in the Côte d'Azur for the last three years.'

She smiled. 'That sounds like a tough gig—all that glamour and money, the jet-set lifestyle.'

'I was working in the *arrière-pays,* the back country, the small villages in the hills. Although I did enjoy visiting Monaco and Cannes on my weekends. Who would not?' He grinned, his eyes sparkling with devilment, a hint of a man who enjoyed the good things in life.

His grin sent a helix of heat spiralling through her. How could one smile from a man she'd only just met make her cheeks burn? She tried to sound professional and regain her equilibrium. 'Amaroo is a different planet from Monaco. I bet there are a few cultural shocks in store for you.'

He shrugged again, the relaxed movement flowing from head to toe. 'It makes for an interesting time and I can practise becoming an Aussie again. May I offer you coffee, Charlotte?'

'That would be lovely. Black, please.' The coil of tension inside unwound completely. All her fears were unfounded. He was charming, could laugh at himself, and this was, as she had expected, a casual 'get-to-know-you' session.

He poured the coffee and carried two cups back to the desk.

'Thank you.' She took the proffered cup, breathing in the spicy aroma of the fresh brew.

Xavier rounded his desk. As he sat down he deftly slid the

top folder from the pile. 'Charlotte, I called you in today to discuss the community midwifery programme.' He pulled open the blue folder. 'I believe you're the midwife in charge of this project?'

'Actually, I'm the only midwife involved in the project. However, the plan is to extend the programme at the end of the financial year and employ another midwife.'

'I see.' He took a sip from his coffee, his lean fingers wrapping themselves around the cup. 'As you are probably aware, part of my brief as the new medical director is to review all the hospital's programmes.'

She nodded. 'It's a great way to become familiar with the hospital.'

'And after reading all these files…' he tapped the top of the stack '…your programme stands out.'

Pride and satisfaction bubbled up inside her. 'Thank you.' She sat forward enthusiastically, always ready to talk about her programme, her passion. 'I'm really proud of what's been achieved. It's innovative and cost-effective.'

He put his fingers and thumbs together, creating a diamond shape, and rested his forefingers against his lips. His head moved in an almost imperceptible nod. 'Innovative perhaps, but these women could come into hospital and have their children here where all the facilities exist, *oui*?'

Magnetic dark eyes, warm with persuasion, gazed at her. For the first time she glimpsed in their depths a flash of steely determination.

The rumours she'd heard about this man suddenly jelled in her mind. A bitter taste scalded the back of her mouth.

Keep calm. 'I don't agree. Have you read the mission state-ment?' Charlie reached over and slid the folder off the desk.

She quickly located the paper she was looking for and pushed it back toward him.

She didn't have to read it herself. She'd written every word and they were engraved on her memory. 'To provide women with birthing options. To offer a safe childbirth environment in a non-medical setting to women who satisfy the stringent criteria. To reduce hospital costs and reduce in-patient stays.' She crossed her arms against her thundering heart but kept her voice even. 'You seem to have missed the point, Dr Laurent.'

A muscle twitched in his jaw but his face remained calm and the expression friendly. 'I think, Charlotte, perhaps you have missed *my* point.' His rich voice contained a slight coolness that hadn't been there before. 'Your programme is a duplication of existing services. Which means "cost-effective" it is not.'

Her fatigue instantly disappeared. Indignation kicked in. 'How can it be a duplication of services when it isn't copying a service provided by the hospital?'

His hand tensed. 'Women have a service. They have an obstetric unit geared to cope with all the complications that can occur in childbirth.'

'They have a medical model that isn't what all women want!' The words shot out sharp and loud, despite her resolve to keep calm. She must make him understand.

Rising quickly from her chair, she strode across to the large bookshelves that lined one wall. 'Here.' She grabbed a thick volume from the shelf.

Turning back toward the desk, she almost collided with him. The plush carpet had absorbed any noise made by his footsteps when he'd followed her to the bookshelves. Close up his height dwarfed her, her head barely reaching his shoulder. His aromatic citrus aftershave swirled around her, filling her nostrils. She stifled the urge to breathe in deeply.

She quickly stepped around him, needing to put a great deal of space between them. Needing to get her hammering heart under control. She'd never reacted to a man like this before. It had to be exhaustion.

Clutching the bound copy of the report to her chest, she marched back to the desk. 'Are you familiar with the state review of birthing services? I think perhaps you were in France when it was conducted.'

She restrained herself from slamming it down on the desk. Instead, she clung to every shred of reason and logic she could muster, desperate to keep a lid on her ever-growing fears for her programme. 'Much of Michel Odent's philosophy became the benchmark for the recommendations of the report.

'As a fellow Frenchman, I'm sure you're completely *au fait* with his work. Here in Amaroo we started putting the recommendations into action.' She sat down.

Xavier followed suit. 'Charlotte, I can see you are passionate about your project and passion is a wonderful thing.' His eyes sparkled and a hint of a smile tugged at his mouth, giving it a sensual look.

Her gaze zeroed in on his lips, almost mesmerised. She forced herself to blink and swallowed hard. *What the hell was wrong with her?*

Enough! She squared her shoulders. 'I've worked very hard these last twelve months to get this project off the ground. I really believe in it.'

'I'm sure you do.' He leaned back into his black leather chair. 'Was this project a board initiative?'

'No, I approached Dr Carson with the idea and he took it to the board under his recommendation.'

'I see.' He ran his long fingers across his jaw.

Panic started to build. 'I'm not sure you do.' She took in a deep breath and tried to speak calmly. 'Based on the review, interviewing the women of the community and taking into account Dr Carson's workload, this programme filled everyone's needs.'

Her patients deserved this programme. All her hard work, the long hours, everything she did—she did with her patients' wellbeing in mind.

He pulled out a piece of paper covered in figures. 'It does not matter how much you believe this programme is needed if there is no money available to run it.'

Economic rationalist. The hospital gossip ran through her head. 'Dr Laurent, there's a lot more to running an obstetric unit than financial figures on a page. In Amaroo people matter, they are not just numbers and throughput. Since you arrived have you spotted a patient? Spoken to any pregnant women and heard what they want? Or are you so engrossed in your precious figures that you've forgotten the whole point of why the hospital exists?'

She heard his sharp intake of breath. Had she touched a nerve? Good.

He suddenly sat forward and drummed his fingers against the notepad on the desk. The noise echoed around the office, bouncing off the suffocating tension that hung in the air.

He finally spoke, weariness tinging his words. 'I have taken on this job only to discover the hospital has a huge financial deficit. If this community is to continue to have a hospital, we have to rein in spending. I'm sure you agree with me that the loss of the hospital would be tragic.'

'Absolutely.' At least they agreed on one thing.

'You seem so certain in your belief that the outreach midwifery programme is vital to the women of this community.

I am yet to be convinced.' A look of irony crossed his face. 'However, as you so eloquently point out, I have yet to fully investigate the programme.' He leaned forward, his elbows resting on the desk. 'So, as from today, your programme is under review.'

Charlie's coffee turned to acid in her stomach. 'Exactly what does "review" mean?'

He raised his brows. 'It means detailed reports, regular meetings and close supervision.'

Her heart banged against her ribs in agitation. 'And who is going to work the crazy hours I do and supervise me?'

His dark gaze found hers, creating a hypnotic effect. '*Moi*. I will.'

Her breath stalled in her throat, trapping all words.

'Believe me, Charlotte, this is the best way. By the time I have finished examining this *programme*, I'll know everything there is to know. And then I will make my decision about the future of community midwifery. This is a fair solution, is it not?'

Her heart pounded. Her brain struggled, railing against this pronouncement. Hating his logic and yet knowing that it was eminently fair. 'I... Yes, I guess it is.'

'Good. I look forward to seeing you at nine tomorrow morning.' He gave a quiet yet determined smile. 'Unless, of course, there is a baby between now and then.'

'You wish to be called at two a.m.?' Disbelief laced her words.

'*Certainement.* My secretary will give you my pager and mobile phone number.'

He stood up, his height unfolding and filling the room.

She stood as well, trying to match his power play.

He walked around the desk, his arm extended as if to say, 'After you.'

She walked toward the door, her mind racing, trying to anticipate his next move.

'Until tomorrow, Charlotte.'

Suddenly she was on the other side of the door, facing the severe glare of the secretary. Frustration collided with admiration. She'd just been dismissed in the most charming way possible.

She was on the back foot. She hated that.

Xavier watched Charlotte leave his office. He hadn't been expecting a midwife with such determination. Neither had he been expecting a curvaceous redhead with long, mud-splattered legs.

And none of that improved his humour.

He ran his forefinger across his jaw and walked across to the window. The ocean shimmered in the summer sunshine, not a wave in sight. Beautiful.

This rugged coastline seemed almost uninhabited compared with the Côte d'Azur. Although he loved his native home, he found the comparative isolation of this part of the world refreshing and restorative to the soul.

And he desperately needed some of that restoration right now. Not that it looked like it would happen any time soon.

When he'd been approached about this position in Amaroo, he'd jumped on it. His life in France had become untenable and the offer of a job in an area close to his parents and nieces and nephews had seemed almost too good to be true. He'd lost his dream of his own family, so the idea of being close to his extended family gave him a sense of connectedness.

This job had given him the opportunity to come to the other side of the world and start over. Leave the northern hemisphere and the mess that was his personal life behind and get established 'down under'.

But nothing ran smoothly.

The telephone interview had glossed over the fact the hospital board had just been sacked for financial mismanagement. He'd arrived to find a financial mess and a hospital on the brink of closure. So, instead of dividing his time between patient care and administration, he was chained to his desk. He had the Department of Health demanding he make radical changes to pull the budget into line and get the hospital back on track.

He sighed. Having bureaucrats breathing down his throat was galling enough. He didn't need Charlotte Buchanan inferring he was a soulless, uncaring number-cruncher.

He cared. He loved his work—loved delivering babies and watching new families take shape. *Zut!* He wasn't the bad guy here. But he had a budget to fix and he wanted it fixed *now*.

Only then could he get on with his life. His new Australian life.

He picked up his white coat and made his way down to the antenatal clinic. He was looking forward to some hands-on medicine. It made a pleasant change from balance sheets.

And he needed to *do something* after his encounter with the tenacious yet stunning Charlotte. Attraction had arced between them like electricity, jolting him to his core.

Once before he'd been attracted to a woman who had been so tied up in her job that nothing else and no one else had mattered. She'd marched through his heart wearing jackboots. He wasn't taking that road again. Ever.

He strode down the corridor, shaking his head to get rid of the vision of emerald-green eyes that sparkled with passion. It was passion for her job, nothing else. He'd do well to remember that.

CHAPTER TWO

CHARLIE drove into the car park, her daily dose of awe whizzing through her at the fact she got to work in a place where she could see whales cavorting in the ocean. For a moment she sat staring out to sea through binoculars, watching a sleek black mammal fling all ninety tonnes of itself out of the ocean.

Every year the whales came to Amaroo to give birth and raise their calves. She liked the symmetry. While the whales were birthing, she was helping the women of Amaroo do the same thing. Over the years the whales had faced many battles for survival, and now it looked like she faced a survival battle herself.

Putting the binoculars away, she slung her bag over her shoulder and headed toward the midwifery building, stifling a yawn.

Her desperate craving for sleep hadn't been met. Instead, she'd tossed all night, images of piercing black eyes interspersed with a recurring slamming door meaning she'd woken up tired and groggy.

Dr Xavier Laurent wanted to close down community midwifery, did he? Well, just let him try.

She straightened her shoulders. It was needed, it was valid, it was…her.

All she'd ever wanted to do was bring babies into the world to take their place in loving families. Her parents and Richard had never understood that. Never chosen to understand.

She pushed the pain of their rejection away. It achieved nothing.

She knew the deal. She'd had to fight for her career once before. It looked like she'd have to do it again. She'd start by running an efficient antenatal clinic. The clinic would be the perfect place to showcase her skills and the merits of the programme.

She'd dazzle him with her skills and professionalism.

Don't let him dazzle you. She shook her head against the traitorous thought. Yesterday she'd been caught off guard. Today she came armour plated, completely immune to a lilting French accent and magnetic charm. Dr Laurent was nothing more than her boss. She mentally put him in the 'boss box' in her head.

She jogged up the old, worn steps of the midwifery clinic, feeling the coolness from the old bricks against her skin. In summer, the thick walls gave welcome relief from the heat and the large verandas caught any passing sea breeze. The exterior of the midwifery building had an old-world charm, which contrasted with the modern, welcoming interior. A home away from home for pregnant women.

Charlie dropped her bag into the bottom of the filing cabinet in her office and slammed it shut. 'Right.' She started working through her mental list of tasks to be achieved before nine a.m. When Xav—Dr Laurent turned up he would find the consummate professional.

She heard the front door creak open.

Her heart almost bounced out of her chest. Damn, the man was early.

A pale, wan face peeked around the office door. 'Charlie, have you got a minute?'

Relief flooded into every pore. She was always ready for patients. 'Sure have. Come in.' Charlie quickly swung a chair out for Melissa, whose anxiety preceded her into the office.

'Oh, Charlie, I feel just awful.' Melissa moaned, and her eyes filled with tears. 'I can't keep anything down. I've never had morning sickness like this before.'

Charlie patted her hand, sympathetically. 'I know it's awful, but the good news is that you're actually feeling sick.'

Melissa looked up incredulously. 'How can it be good?'

'Morning sickness is a good indication that this pregnancy is a strong healthy embryo. Your pregnancy hormones are high and they're making you feel sick. We just have to help you get through the next few weeks.' Charlie smiled reassuringly at Melissa. 'Can anyone help you out, minding little Jake for a couple of hours in the afternoons?'

'John's mum has offered, but I thought I would be all right.' Melissa blew her nose and wiped her face.

'So take up the offer and have an afternoon's sleep. Morning sickness is always worse when you are tired. Ginger tablets are really helpful for the nausea and so is vitamin B6.'

She reached out and touched her arm. 'Believe me, Melissa, the morning sickness will fade.'

Melissa gave a wry laugh. 'Let's hope it finishes before the baby is born.'

Twenty-five minutes later Melissa left and Charlie quickly assembled the medical histories in order of appointment. She was ready to greet Xav—Dr Laurent.

The loud and piercing beep of her pager sounded at the same moment it vibrated against her. She quickly checked the digital read-out. Accident and Emergency? A surge of adrenaline shot through her. She could count on one hand the amount of times she had been paged to go to A and E.

In her line of work she saw the uncomplicated, straightforward pregnancies. Her programme had rigid guidelines as to who could be admitted and all high-risk pregnancies were excluded.

She quickly scribbled a note apologising to her clients for the delay of the start of clinic. As she pushed the pin into the wood, the ramifications of the page hit her. Xavier Laurent would have to wait before he could start her supervision. Relief mingled with adrenaline, the combination making her feel quite odd. She'd phone him from A and E and delay his visit.

Xavier pushed himself away from his desk, his stomach growling. Breakfast was a distant memory. He'd done his rounds at seven a.m., enjoying his 'patient fix' so he could squeeze in an hour of paperwork before his first appointment.

He checked his watch. 9:05 a.m. *Zut!* Not enough time to make coffee. He was late already to meet Charlotte Buchanan. Her programme looked to be superfluous and with money tight he needed to avoid two services offering the same thing. But convincing her of that wouldn't be easy. The woman's zealous approach to her job seemed almost unhealthy.

So much passion. Too much passion for his peace of mind. An image of her alabaster face swam into his mind, quickly followed by a vivid picture of her toned, shapely legs and narrow waist that begged to be cupped by large hands.

Never again would he confuse passion for work with love. Genevieve had torn the scales from his eyes and a piece from his heart. Her career aspirations had come ahead of everything—patients, their unborn child, him. He hated that it had taken him so long to work that out. That lives had been lost.

His pager beeped, snapping him back to reality. Obstetric emergency. Two lives at stake.

He grabbed his white coat and stethoscope, a charge of adrenaline skimming along his veins. The quickest way to A and E was across the lawn quadrangle. Dodging the timed sprinklers, he ran across the square, arriving at the entrance the exact moment as Charlotte.

She'd been running as well and her chest heaved against her blouse, the fabric moving smoothly across her pert breasts. Her cheeks blushed pink and her pupils, now large black discs against an emerald backdrop, gave her a sensual glow that hovered around her like an aura. She flicked her damp hair back from her face and licked the droplets of sprinkler water from her lips.

White heat blazed through him.

He cleared his throat, pushing the unwanted reaction away, forcing himself to regain control. He pushed open the large Perspex doors. 'After you.'

She ducked under his arm, her perfume filling his nostrils with the scent of wild roses.

Helen Bannister, the unit manager, met them with gowns and gloves, which she thrust at them. 'Sharon Jenkins is on her way in with shoulder-tip pain. I thought you'd want to be here, Charlie.

'We're frantic at the moment with walking wounded. I've cleared the resuscitation room for you and the ambulance will be here soon. Medical Records is bringing her history over, but in the meantime, Dr Laurent, Charlie will fill you in.' Helen briskly walked away.

'Come.' Xavier strode quickly into the resuscitation room

to prepare, his triage training coming to the fore. If he had some time to set up, hopefully the emergency would run as smoothly as something totally unpredictable could.

He turned to ask Charlotte a question but the words died on his lips. The enticing glow on her face had faded, replaced by an almost frightening whiteness, which emphasised a smattering of freckles across the bridge of her nose.

Her pallor, so sudden and unexpected, worried him. She didn't look well at all. 'Are you all right? Do you need to leave and lie down?'

'No.' She nibbled her plump bottom lip.

His groin tightened. *Alors.* His reaction to this woman was insane. Unwanted.

She reached for the intravenous set, her concentration centred on priming the unit. 'I'm fine, really.' Her voice sounded soft and uncertain—a contrast to her firm tones of yesterday.

He dragged his gaze from her kissable mouth, shaken by his reaction to her. He was a doctor. It was time to act like one. 'It sounds like an ectopic pregnancy and a rupture of the Fallopian tube. What can you tell me about the patient?'

She sighed, her breath shuddering out of her lungs. 'Sharon Jenkins is a thirty-four-year-old woman with a long history of infertility due to pelvic inflammatory disease. This is her first pregnancy.'

Blood pounded in his head. Suddenly the pallor of her face made sense. She was one hundred per cent well but her patient was not.

Bile burned the back of his throat. His chest tightened with rage. With PID, Sharon Jenkins would fall outside the guidelines of the outreach programme. Had Charlotte stooped so low as to risk a patient's life to boost numbers for her beloved programme?

He clenched his fist. In France he'd been naïve, totally missing the signs of driving ambition. But never again. Today he saw the signs flashing brightly and harshly, like neon against a black sky.

What was it with some professional women that made them behave like barracudas? How could ambition blind people to their professional obligations? How could they forget their oath of 'Do no harm'?

Anger swirled in his gut, revisiting past hurt. He didn't need a midwife who put her career ahead of her patients in *his* hospital.

He flicked on the ECG machine and tested the electrodes, the familiar action tamping down his anger. Now wasn't the time to deal with this. Right now all his attention needed to be zeroed in on his patient. But the moment the emergency was over, Charlotte Buchanan and her programme would no longer be part of his hospital.

The doors swung open and the ambulance officers hurriedly wheeled in the gurney. Sharon lay on her side, her face grey and contorted in pain. Her skin glistening with the sheen of sweat.

Charlie raced to her side. 'I'm here, Sharon.' Concern filled her voice and she took the woman's hand, giving it a supportive squeeze.

Xavier swallowed the derisive sound that rose in his throat. Charlotte had good reason for concern. She could be struck off the nursing register for defying guidelines and putting a patient at risk.

He turned his attention to his patient. 'Mrs Jenkins, I am Dr Laurent, the obstetrician who will be looking after you.'

Sharon's fear-filled eyes focused on his face. 'My shoulder hurts so much, Doctor. I feel like I'm going to vomit.'

Charlie silently produced a kidney dish, tucking it under Sharon's arm.

'I'm sorry you feel so unwell. I'm going to have to examine you but I will be as gentle as I can.' He smiled at her, hoping it might distract her for a moment. 'At least in this heat, my hands are warm, *oui*?'

He methodically examined her abdomen. Guarded, distended and bloated, it fitted the picture of intra-peritoneal bleeding. Such bleeding caused the referred, shoulder-tip pain.

'Her blood pressure is eighty on fifty. I'll insert the drip.'

Charlotte's voice broke through his concentration, her words mirroring his thoughts. Like most ambitious people she was supremely competent and good at her job. It was the 'take-no-prisoners' approach he objected to.

He gave a curt nod. 'Take blood for cross-matching and put up a Haemaccel infusion once you've got the line established.'

'Right.' She grabbed the Haemaccel from the fridge and then paused before acting, explaining the procedure to Sharon. 'I'm going to put a tourniquet around your arm and then put a needle into your vein so we can give you some fluid.'

Xavier picked up the phone and rang Theatre, organising Sharon's immediate transfer upstairs. While he waited for Kristy Sanders to confirm an anaesthetist, he watched Charlotte. Surprise filled him at the ease in which she inserted the IV into their shocked patient. Sharon was in venous shutdown—it would have been a challenging job to find a vein, let alone achieve in-venation so quickly. Grudging respect for her skills edged in.

'Kristy, tell Phillip I need him in Theatre now.' He hung up and turned to look at his patient. Charlie deftly stripped nail polish from Sharon's fingers. The tang of acetone stung his nostrils.

He couldn't put it off any longer. He had to break the bad news to Sharon. He hated to be the one to confirm shattered dreams.

He picked up her hand. 'Sharon, I am sorry. It's highly likely that one of your Fallopian tubes has ruptured. The embryo was probably growing inside your tube instead of settling into your uterus. We will do an ultrasound upstairs in Theatre to confirm my diagnosis, but I am certain I am right and I need to operate to stop the bleeding.'

Sharon gripped his hand. 'Will I lose the baby?'

His heart contracted at the pain his words would inflict. *'Je suis désolé.'* The French slipped out instinctively. 'I am so sorry.'

The woman crumbled, sobs racking her body, her grip on his hand vice-like. 'Has…has someone rung my husband?'

Xavier found this part of being an obstetrician the most difficult. For the most part it was an extremely happy job but when a pregnancy went wrong he experienced some of his patient's pain.

Charlie spoke quietly to Sharon, her voice gentle and calming. 'We have to get you up to Theatre now, but Bob is on his way in and he'll be waiting for you in the ward after the surgery is over. Dr Laurent will explain everything to him after the surgery and then again to you when you're up to hearing it.'

She glanced at him, her gaze hooking his, almost a plea in her eyes.

The look completely confused him. He shrugged it away. His patient needed all his concentration.

Sharon's crying jag eased to shuddering sniffs. She transferred her grip from Xavier's hands to Charlie's. 'Oh, Charlie…'

'I know.' She blinked rapidly, her eyes deepening in colour with the shine of tears. She squeezed Sharon's hand again as the porter arrived to take her to Theatre. 'I'll see you after surgery.'

Stepping back, she watched the trolley disappear out into the corridor.

Bitter rage imploded inside him as he watched this charade of caring. She'd deliberately put Sharon at risk, ignoring her professional duties, putting her ambition first.

'You're coming to Theatre with your patient, Ms Buchanan.' The words rolled out on a growl.

Her eyes widened. 'But I…'

He ignored the shocked look on her face. 'But nothing. I need a skilled assistant and you are that person.' He needed her technical skills, but just as importantly, *she* needed to see first hand the damage her ambition had caused. Sharon would lose a Fallopian tube, and if the other tube was damaged her only chance of future pregnancy would be in vitro fertilisation.

'Fine.' A thread of determination edged into her voice, the same determination he'd heard yesterday. It completely overrode the emotion he'd seen in her eyes and the tone she'd used when she'd spoken with Sharon.

That didn't surprise him. She'd been caught off guard for a moment, but now she'd pulled herself together.

No doubt her mind raced with how she could save her skin. And her programme. Well, no amount of fast talking would get her out of her own mess. Staff acting in a non-professional manner didn't belong in his hospital.

Ten minutes later he strode into Theatre. 'Ready, Phillip?'

'Ready my end.' The anaesthetist glanced up from his dials and screens.

'*Bien.* Scalpel.'

A pair of emerald eyes flashed at him over a mask. Charlotte silently slapped the scalpel into his outstretched palm.

He made the incision and quickly located the ruptured Fallopian tube. Sharon's pelvic cavity was a mess of blood and adhesions. It took all his concentration to stem the bleeding and try to save what he could.

Every time he opened his mouth to ask for an instrument or suction, Charlotte anticipated him. She organised the scout nurse for silk and extra packs. He had no reason to request anything.

The co-ordination of the surgical team was seamless under her steady guidance. He could feel the respect the staff had for her. Could he have missed something?

He overruled the thought.

They might be blind but he refused to be duped. He knew her type inside and out. Her tunnel-vision focus for her job and programme had made her commit a professional sin.

The moment Sharon Jenkins was in Recovery, Charlotte Buchanan would be escorted from the hospital.

He gently probed the other tube. 'We'll run some dye through this just to check it's patent.'

He studied the screen, watching the dye travelling easily down a straighter Fallopian tube with no sign of obstruction.

'Oh, thank goodness.' The words, barely audible, breathed out from behind Charlotte's mask.

For the first time since coming into surgery she looked at him. Relief and joy mingled in her eyes. He'd expected the relief. But the joy threw him. That look of happiness in her eyes wasn't for herself, but for Sharon.

For a brief moment he held her gaze, savouring the satisfaction of a lucky save and some good surgery. Then he remembered the great danger in which her ambition had placed Sharon.

'Four-O silk.' He almost grabbed the suture from her gloved hand as his anger surged again at her unprofessional behaviour. To steady himself he focused on creating small neat stitches along Sharon's abdomen.

'Thanks, Phillip.' He turned toward the anaesthetist. 'You can bring her round now.' He stripped off his gloves and stepped back from the operating table. 'Ms Buchanan, I wish to see you in the prep room.'

Surprise crossed her now unmasked face. She dropped the mask in the linen skip. 'I'll be back soon to help you clean up, Kristy.'

The scout nurse nodded and watched with interest as Xavier opened the door and ushered Charlie into the adjoining room.

All the anger and frustration he'd worked so hard at keeping under control for two hours exploded. '*Mon Dieu!* What were you thinking? How could you put a patient with a history like that in your programme?' He thrust his hands out in front of him, gesticulating his complete lack of understanding. He struggled to find the English words he needed, his mind racing in French.

'You have overstepped the mark. I have no choice but to close your programme. It is defunct. Finished. People who put their job before their patients do not belong in my hospital.'

He expected raging fury, a barrage of words. But he got neither. A myriad of emotions darted across her face, incredulity the most prominent. When she finally spoke the only emotion he could detect was tiredness.

'Sharon Jenkins isn't my patient.'

The words punched him in the chest, winding him. *Hein?* He shook his head. 'What?'

She raised her head slightly her chin jutting forward. 'Sharon Jenkins isn't my patient.' Her quiet words shot into the strained silence. 'She is a very dear friend.'

Confusion swamped him, his thoughts jumbled and incoherent. 'But they paged you to attend A and E?'

She looked at him as if he were a bewildered child and sighed. 'This is a small town, Dr Laurent. Everyone knows everybody and their problems. Helen knew Sharon would want me to be with her.'

His brain, normally quick to comprehend, wrestled valiantly to come to grips with this new information. He'd been so certain of her negligence, so secure in his conviction of her. So quick to see her as guilty.

He was so wrong.

She stood before him, her head tilted slightly to one side, with the light catching her hair, sending shafts of golden red swirling around her. Luminous. Truly beautiful.

He didn't want to see her that way. Not as a woman. He had enough battles on his hands getting the hospital under control without being attracted to another woman who lived for her job. He would not risk brutal duplicity again.

It would be so much easier if she were gone. Out of his hospital. Out of his thoughts.

But the balance of power had just shifted. How could he have so misread the situation? How had he got it so totally and utterly wrong? He hauled in a deep breath. 'I see.'

In his rush to find her guilty he'd lost perspective. He'd let his pain of betrayal colour his judgement. In his desire to find a quick solution to his budget problems he'd acted hastily.

He'd never stopped to consider her as a person with a network of friends in the town. He cleared his throat. Humble pie didn't taste very palatable. 'I seem to have misconstrued your relationship with Mrs Jenkins.'

She raised her eyebrows and remained silent, her body rigid with tension.

He struggled not to sound so formal, wishing he could apologise in French. He chose honesty instead. 'I acted on emotion, not facts. I let the past interfere in a place it does not belong. I am truly sorry, Charlotte.'

She moved slowly, pushing off the bench she'd been leaning against, her eyes round with resignation and disappointment. For a brief moment her shoulders drooped but she quickly straightened, standing tall. 'I accept your apology.'

The coolness of her voice told him he had not been forgiven. She turned and walked toward the door.

He moved quickly, needing to explain.

They reached the door at the same moment, their hands colliding on the handle.

Fire on ice.

He heard her sharp intake of breath as she quickly withdrew her hand, her cheeks pink.

He caught her gaze, her flashing eyes full of questions and confusion.

'One moment, *s'il vous plaît.* Please, I have something more I need to say.'

'Shoot.' She took a step back, crossing her arms across her chest.

The colloquial expression confused him. '*Pardon?* I am not in the habit of shooting my staff.'

For a brief moment the trace of a smile flit across her face. 'Please, go on.'

He concentrated on his words, hauling his mind back from

chasing her smile. 'I wish to start our working relationship again. I have not been fair to you. I give you my commitment that I will review your programme using the birthing services review guidelines as well as our budget requirements.'

'Good.' Her face remained impassive.

'Good?' He'd expected more than that.

'Good. I'm very glad you are a fair man. Now, if you would please stand aside, I need to go and tell Bob Jenkins that his wife is in Recovery. I expect you will wish to speak to him too.'

She moved passed him out into the corridor, her theatre greens not able to hide the curvaceous lines that lay beneath them.

He slammed the door closed. She drew him like a firefly to light. But if he went down that road he would be scorched. He'd read her reports, detailing her activities of the last six months. The amount of time she spent at work left no room for anything else in her life. Her commitment was total.

Why was he even thinking about her like this? Relationships with colleagues burned and he wasn't putting his hand up for that experience again. And it wasn't just his experience. He'd watched friends' relationships fail as they'd tried to carve out careers and keep relationships afloat.

No way was he acting on an attraction that would take him down a dead-end, heart-wrenching road again. He wasn't that stupid.

He slammed his hands in his pockets, his fingers curling around a piece of paper.

He pulled it out and smiled at the reminder. Phil Carson's party. After the day he'd had the party would be the perfect event to push all thought of work and Charlotte Buchanan out of his mind.

CHAPTER THREE

CHARLIE sank back against the cold metal of the lockers in the theatre changing room, letting the coolness flood into her overheated body. She closed her eyes but Xavier's tanned face invaded her thoughts, reviving the flame of desire his hand on hers had sparked. A flame that had heated every inch of her, igniting parts of her body she'd thought had died long ago from lack of use.

And she hated that.

Hated that her body would betray her at the hint of sophisticated charm and an intoxicating accent.

She drew in a long, steadying breath and focused on the facts. Facts flattened desire. She needed as many facts as she could get.

He'd thought her capable of deliberately putting a patient's life at risk. Her heart pounded at the thought. How could he have thought that of her? What had she done that would make him think so badly of her? She hugged herself, trying to make sense of the situation. His accusation had rocked her to her marrow.

Yesterday she'd defended her programme, asked him to give it a fair go. She'd done no more than anybody else who believed in what they did. No one wanted to see their hard efforts go down the drain.

She rubbed her temples. His accusation made no sense.

'I let the past interfere in a place it does not belong.' The image of his handsome Gallic features paling under his tan as he'd spoken stayed with her, intriguing her. Was the past he'd spoken of the reason he'd come back to Australia? What had happened in his past to make him jump so quickly to an incorrect conclusion? She really wanted to know more.

She shook her head. His past had nothing to do with her. He was an excellent doctor—his treatment of Sharon both surgically and as a caring physician had been faultless. She'd been impressed by how he'd handled the medical side of the emergency from start to finish.

As for his accusation, well, he'd genuinely apologised and requested to start their working relationship again. His contrition and fairness had shone through. For the sake of her patients she'd do everything in her power to work co-operatively with Xavier.

The shimmering sensations that swamped her whenever she was near him—those she would simply ignore.

Charlie hummed as she drove the short distance to the Carson farm, smiling at her golden Labrador, Spanner, who hung her head out the window, tongue lolling, taking in all the smells of summer.

The warm evening declared itself the perfect venue for a party. Hearing Marie Carson's voice on her answering-machine, inviting her to an impromptu barbecue, had been the perfect antidote to a horrid day. Charlie adored the Carsons and had missed them desperately while they'd been touring, celebrating Phil's overdue retirement. Now they were home and in typical style were throwing a party.

Charlie intended to let her hair down and drive away the

vestiges of the day, including all thoughts of work and Dr Xavier Laurent.

Spanner barked as she turned into the long gravel driveway lined with agapanthus, their large white and purple heads swaying gently in the breeze. The Carsons' rambling homestead seemed more like home to Charlie than her parents' house ever had.

Phil and Marie had taken her under their wing when she'd first arrived in Amaroo, offering her friendship. She'd waited for the inevitable suggestions, the subtle attempts at moulding her, directing her life. They'd never come. For the first time in her life she'd found acceptance. She treasured it dearly.

Kids and dogs charged around the home paddock. Charlie opened the door to let her eager dog out. 'Off you go, Span.'

'Hey, Charlie!' Jenny and Robert Martin, both school teachers, called to her from the volleyball court. 'Join us. We need some help.' The ball sailed passed them, landing on the baseline.

Charlie laughed and held up a bottle of wine. 'Be there as soon as I've said hi to Phil.' A small thrill shot through her. She loved being part of this community. She followed the aroma of barbecued onions, her stomach gurgling. Lunch seemed a long time ago.

Standing behind the barbecue in the most ridiculous apron she'd ever seen stood Phil, expertly grilling steak. He waved the tongs in her direction. 'It's about time you showed up, Charlie. Working too hard, I presume?'

Charlie gave him a hug. 'Of course not. Would I do that?' She laughed. 'Where on earth did you get that apron?'

'You need a tacky souvenir of every holiday and this fitted all the criteria and then some.' His smile increased as he caught sight of his wife. 'Marie, look who finally showed up.'

A well-groomed woman in her sixties hurried over to embrace her. 'You look tired, dear. Has there been a baby boom?'

'You know how it is.' Charlie was deliberately vague. A party was not the place to open her heart to Marie about a certain black-haired doctor with dark penetrating eyes whose arrival had caused her chaos, both professionally and personally.

'Come along, then, let's get some food into you.' Marie picked up a plate and started loading it with salad and some of the home-grown steak that was grilled to perfection.

Charlie joined a group of friends under a market umbrella, eating the wonderful food, sipping her wine and letting the conversation wrap around her in a convivial way. The day's tensions slipped away, and she relaxed for the first time since meeting Xavier.

'Charlie.'

She swivelled around. Marie walked toward her with her arm happily tucked into the crook of Xavier's.

Her breath swooshed out of her lungs as her blood rushed to her feet. In a suit he'd had an aura of sophistication and control. In soft linen trousers with a sky-blue shirt and braided leather sandals on his feet, he radiated a devastating careless style.

She tried to breathe.

How could she have been so stupid? Of course, she should have realised. This was Xavier Laurent's welcome party as well. She wanted to sink under the table and out of view. But there was nothing she could do except stand, smile and act as though nothing in her world had changed.

Anything less and she'd face an inquisition from Marie.

She desperately hoped her body's crazy lust-fuelled reaction to the gorgeous doctor didn't show on her face.

* * *

Charlotte. Xavier blinked and swallowed an embarrassed groan as the enigmatic midwife rose gracefully to her feet. It had never occurred to him that the person Marie Carson insisted he meet would be the one woman he wasn't quite ready to face.

His behaviour earlier that day still haunted him. He couldn't believe he'd let his hurt from the fallout of his past cloud his professional judgement. He prided himself on being objective at all times. He'd convinced himself he'd left the past in France, where it belonged. Instead, he'd used it against a co-worker, a woman.

When he'd left work that afternoon he'd believed he had at least seventeen hours for his apology to take effect. Seventeen hours before he had to face Charlotte again, and even then it would be with the safety buffer of work between them.

But perhaps a social situation was the ideal place to really make amends. Show her he wasn't an ogre, establish a working friendship. He'd chat with her and then head back to Alison Richards, the kindergarten teacher he'd been chatting to when Marie had brought him over to meet Charlotte.

Alison had seemed a sensible woman, the type of woman he should be noticing. Someone who didn't work in medicine.

He smiled a welcome and inclined his head in greeting. 'Charlotte, good evening. It's lovely to see you.'

'Xavier.' She matched the tilt of his head with one of her own—her luminous eyes filled with caution.

A twinge of guilt shot through him. He was the cause of that hesitancy.

Marie seemed oblivious to the tension that radiated from Charlie. 'Xavier, Charlie is like the daughter we never had.

And, Charlie, did you know that Xavier's mother and I are very dear friends?'

Without really waiting for an answer from either of them, Marie suddenly turned to leave. 'Oh, dear, Phil's waving madly from the barbecue so he must need a hand. Well, you don't need me—the two of you will have loads in common. Oh, and, Charlie, be a dear and introduce him to the others.' With a quick pat on both their arms she walked briskly away.

Xavier caught a flash of apprehension cross Charlotte's face. The guilt twisted in deeper. 'I imagine that to disobey Marie's instructions to talk would be tantamount to treason.' He grinned, hoping to put her at ease.

Her face relaxed and her eyes suddenly sparkled with laughter. 'You're spot on there. Marie likes to bring people together.'

Her vibrancy surrounded him, drawing him toward her like a moth to a flame. He sought her gaze. 'Then perhaps I should thank her as I am not certain you would wish to have talked to me this evening if she had not insisted.'

She gave him a wry smile. 'Amaroo is too small a town to hold a grudge, Xavier. I can forgive you one lapse of judgement.' She raised her brows, her emerald eyes dancing as she looked him up and down. 'But just one, mind. Next time it happens you could end up helping Phil here on the farm, mucking out the pigpen. I'm sure the pigs would love Armani.'

His laughter joined hers, the two tones mixing melodically, warming him. 'Ah, but I was raised on a farm, Charlotte. I spent many hours discussing my adolescent crushes with the pigs—they are good listeners.'

He laughed at her wide-eyed look, enjoying the fact that he didn't fit into whatever pigeonhole she had tried to place him in her mind. Enjoying the fact they could tease each other in a friendly, platonic way.

'Charlie, we're waiting for you!' Robert Martin, red-faced and panting, ran over from the volleyball match. 'We're down five points and we need your setting skills.'

Charlie hesitated for a moment, glancing behind her at the group at the table, obviously torn between her desire to play volleyball and her promise to Marie to introduce Xavier to the group. 'I'll be there soon.'

'You said that half an hour ago, and we need you now.' Robert bent over to put his hands on his thighs and to catch his breath.

Xavier didn't want to be the reason Charlotte missed out on playing volleyball. He could meet the other guests later. He put his hand on the panting man's back. 'Robert, I used to play volleyball at Sydney University. May I join you, too?'

He heard Charlotte's gasp of surprise behind him.

Robert straightened up, as if propelled by new life. 'Great! Come on, then, you two, Jenny's waiting for us.'

'So you played at uni?' Charlotte walked beside him to the court. A wicked smile lit up her face, matching the sparkling gleam of competition in her eyes. 'Now, that would have been a while ago, wouldn't it?'

He laughed. '*Mais oui,* but it is a game also played in France.'

Jenny Martin urged them onto the court. 'Hurry up, you lot! We're seven down now.'

'Coming.' Charlotte paused for a moment by the side of the court, pulling her blouse over her head to reveal a cropped sports top. The black Lycra moulded her breasts, outlining every curve.

Desire shot through him, the complete anthesis of platonic.

What was it about this woman? Every time he convinced himself he was immune to her, his body let him down. Thank goodness for some physical activity. He'd play the game and then find Alison Richards.

He nodded a greeting to the other players, noticing that Charlotte knew them all by name. Just like in Theatre that afternoon. She belonged here. She had what he wanted, what he sought from Amaroo. A sense of belonging.

Robert issued directions. 'You can both start off at the net with Chris. Charlie, you go in the middle, Xavier on the left, and Jenny, Geoff and I'll protect the back.' He headed to the baseline to serve.

Xavier took his position, his skin tingling in awareness of Charlotte standing beside him. Totally aware of the brief Lycra top, and now bike shorts which had magically appeared from under her skirt, emphasising long shapely legs. He gave thanks she wasn't dressed in the traditional skimpy bikini, beach volleyball outfit. He'd never be able to hit the ball.

Focus on the game!

Robert served the ball cleanly and the opposing team returned it in one hit.

'Mine!' Charlie called it, and expertly set the ball up. It sailed high in the air, close to the net.

Xavier jumped, spiking it down on the opposing side, its speed passing all the hands trying to block its passage.

'Yes!' He turned and pushed his arm into the air.

Charlotte smiled broadly, raising her arm and giving him a high five.

A shower of electric shocks carried heat right through him. He quickly pulled his arm back. 'Only twelve points to go.'

The heat of the evening sun bore down on him as it dropped low in the sky. That was why he was hot. It had nothing to do with long legs, swinging auburn hair and flashing emerald eyes.

Le jeu. Focus on the game!

The battle on the court intensified, the opposing side determined to hold onto its lead. A crowd gathered to watch the well-fought match, the gap in the score steadily closing. People took sides, inventing chants as the excitement built.

For the first time since arriving in Amaroo Xavier relaxed. This was why he'd come to the country. To have a life outside work and to belong to a community.

Charlotte whispered conspiratorially. 'We're doing great. Let's keep it up.' Enthusiasm filled her words.

Her aura danced around him, sparkling, enticing him. Did she embrace everything in her life with this much enthusiasm?

'Remember to back up Geoff.'

'Will do.' She gave him a mock salute and a cheeky grin, and spun back to the middle position.

A sense of lightness streaked through him.

'Yours.' Charlotte set the ball.

'Got it!' Xavier spiked it down and won the point, enjoying their teamwork.

The lead narrowed until the score was twenty-four to twenty-three in their favour. One point to win. Adrenaline flowed through Xavier's veins, the thrill of competition giving him a complete buzz. A buzz that had nothing to do with the redhead on his right.

The opposition served a fast ball, which curved down close to the baseline. Geoff dived to dig it up. Charlie pushed the ball up over to Xavier and he leapt to thump it over the net.

The ball was returned, just clearing the net.

Charlie lunged, coming up under the ball to set it up for a

more controlled spike. This time Xavier had time to direct the ball. He powered it back. It landed at the feet of the front-line players.

'Great shot!' Charlotte raised her arms toward him in triumph.

Elation surged through him. He grabbed her around the waist, spinning her around. 'We did it!'

'We did!' Her laughter enveloped him, her arms curved around his shoulders, their touch sparking the flame he'd worked so hard to extinguish with exercise. Heat burned inside him.

For a brief moment he stared into her flushed face, reading joy, elation and an emotion he connected only with Charlotte.

She broke the gaze.

The moment ended.

Robert thumped him on the back, Jenny reached forward to hug him and Geoff and Chris pumped his hand. Almost as quickly the team turned their attention to Charlie and then to the opposition.

Xavier stood catching his breath, watching the antics of an excited group of people celebrating a worthy competition. His gaze followed Charlotte to the sidelines. Mesmerised, he watched her take a long drink of water, her head tilted back, highlighting her long neck. Desire surged, stronger than before.

He refused to listen to it. He would *not* act on it. It was her athleticism he admired. Her skill. She played volleyball like she worked, throwing her heart and soul into it.

She seemed to do everything with such passion. *And if that passion was directed at you?*

He squelched the thought immediately. He knew what worked and what didn't. It was engraved on his soul.

No, it was time to find Alison Richards, the kindergarten

teacher who loved children. He scanned the crowd and saw her standing in a group, silently absorbing the conversation. She seemed small, shy and mousy. No signs of vibrant enthusiasm on her face, no aura of fire and heat surrounding her.

Suddenly fatigue hit him. He really didn't feel like talking to Alison. It was time to head home.

The noise of a distant ringing bell slowly penetrated Charlie's sleep-filled brain. She rolled over and reached for the phone. 'Hello? Charlie Buchanan speaking.' The words tumbled out automatically.

'Charlie, it's David McAllister. Julie's started. Her waters broke about an hour ago.'

Charlie glanced at the clock. Two a.m. 'Was the fluid clear, David?'

'Yes, Charlie.' The experienced father spoke with amusement in his voice. 'You know we would have rung you if it was brownish.'

'Of course you would but it's two in the morning and my brain is just starting to wake up.' She stifled a yawn. 'We'll come straight over. Put the kettle on for me.'

'Don't think you're going to need boiling water for a while yet,' David teased.

'No, but I'm going to need a cup of tea.' She laughed as she hung up the phone. This was the third McAllister baby she would be delivering. The first two had been in hospital but this time the McAllisters had chosen a home birth as part of birth options programme Charlie had introduced.

And this time Xavier would be there, too. She hadn't seen him since the Carsons' party four days ago as he'd been in Theatre or tied up in meetings. But even if she hadn't seen him, he'd taken up residence in her thoughts. Her mind seemed to stream footage of him playing volleyball—long, toned legs, rippling muscles as he jumped to spike the ball, and a wicked smile that made her knees go weak and her heart pound erratically.

She could still feel the touch of his arms around her waist at the end of the match, and the tingling wave of sensations that had built inside her.

She pushed the thoughts away. Even if she were in the market for a relationship, which she wasn't, Xavier was her boss. End of story.

She moved into action. A baby was on the way.

This delivery was her opportunity to prove to him she was the consummate professional and that her programme was a vital part of the midwifery department.

She dialled his number. The phone rang three times before a deep voice resonated down the line, his delicious accent emphasised by the phone. 'Xavier Laurent.'

He didn't even have the decency to sound half-asleep. Instead, his voice held the promise of sensual kisses and a long embrace.

You're the midwife, he's the doctor. Nothing else mattered.

'Xavier, it's Charlotte Buchanan.' What? She never called herself Charlotte. Only her mother called her that.

And Xavier.

One day she was going to kill that inner voice. She straightened her shoulders. This was work. Be professional. 'Julie McAllister's gone into labour. You met her at the antenatal clinic and you wanted to attend the birth. If that's still the case, shall I pick you up on my way to their farm?'

'*Merci,* Charlotte. How long will you be?' Friendliness filled his voice.

She tried to sound a little less businesslike. 'Oh, about ten minutes. I just have to throw some clothes on.' The moment the words came out she wanted to grab them back. She sounded as if she was naked, instead of wearing polka-dot shortie pyjamas.

Low, rumbling laughter came down the line. 'Just as well we are not video-conferencing, eh?' He chuckled. 'See you in ten minutes.'

The line went dead. Charlie's cheeks burned and she knew her face would be bright pink. Blushing at twenty-eight! Heaven help her.

He's the doctor, you're the midwife. Two professionals.

Although it was the middle of the night, the summer air was warm. Charlie pulled on a pair of light cotton trousers and a short-sleeved blouse with the hospital logo embroidered on the pocket.

Grabbing her keys, she gave the slumbering Spanner a pat and went out into the night. A full moon lit the sky and the crickets serenaded the peace of the night. In the distance she heard the slow, rolling waves hitting the shore.

Ten minutes later gravel crunched under her wheels as she pulled into Xavier's driveway. She dimmed her lights as he walked out onto his porch, pulling his front door closed behind him.

Her heartbeat picked up.

Dressed in chinos and a designer polo shirt, he looked far too sexy for the middle of the night. In contrast to her own hair, which she was yet to snag with a ribbon, every strand of his lay in place.

She couldn't help but watch as he walked to the vehicle, his long, confident stride quickly eating up the short distance. He swung up onto the front seat, immediately filling the interior with his long body and citrus aftershave.

She took in a deep breath, more to savour the scent than to steady herself.

'*Bonne Nuit*, Charlotte.' He tilted his head to the side for a moment, his dark eyes scanning her face. Looking into her soul. 'Gorgeous night for a delivery, *n'est-ce pas*?' He snapped his seat belt into place. 'The stars in this country seem to go on for ever.'

'They do, don't they?' Oh, she sounded so inane! 'It's about a twenty-minute drive to the McAllisters'. We just follow the Southern Cross.' She pointed to the distinctive constellation only seen in the southern hemisphere, hanging low in the sky.

Charlie passed him a map, her fingers brushing his. A tendril of longing swept through her and she quickly dropped the map. 'But just in case navigating by the stars isn't specific enough, I thought this might help you become familiar with the area.'

He smiled, straight, white teeth gleaming in the moonlight. '*Merci.*' He flicked on the map light and opened the map, spending the next few minutes studying it.

Charlie reversed out of the driveway and tried to focus on the road and not on the fact that this undeniably gorgeous man sat far too close to her for any peace of mind.

'*Colleague and boss, colleague and boss.*'

'Pardon?' He lifted his head from the map, his black brows raised questioningly.

Surely she'd said that under her breath. She smiled brightly. 'We won't get lost, I know the way.' She gripped the steering-wheel.

Xavier returned to the map. The road rolled on.

His voice broke into her thoughts. 'I was surprised that the hospital offered a home-birth option.'

'Yes, the community was lucky to have Phil Carson.' She smiled fondly. 'He was a man before his time. He'd stand up to the bureaucrats for the things he believed in.'

Charlie heard a mumbled noise beside her and turned her head.

Warring emotions played across Xavier's face. 'He was fortunate to have most of his career untainted by the exploding cost of health care. Things have changed a lot. Now we have to justify every cent and every programme we run.'

A desire to defend her mentor bubbled up inside her. 'True, but that doesn't stop you from fighting for what you believe in. And Phil did that again and again. Amaroo has a great health-care system because of Phil's drive and passion.'

His hands rose palms upward along with his shoulders, a Gallic shrug. 'It also has crippling debt, Charlotte. We cannot ignore that for high ideals.' His volume was soft but the tone determined.

'Julie McAllister could have her baby just as easily in the hospital with the midwives on duty.'

Frustration rushed into her. 'But she deserves to have a choice.'

'She deserves access to quality health care. Amaroo risks losing their hospital if hard choices aren't made and the budget pulled in.' His lips compressed into a straight line.

'I understand that, but why *this* programme? It's based on a cost-effective model. It's safe and gives better outcomes for mothers and babies. Midwife care costs less than hospital-based care. The intervention rate is lower.' She heard her voice rising.

Forcing herself to sound calm, she dropped her voice. 'International studies show the outcomes for planned home births are as safe as hospital births and they are cost-effective.

Australia is lagging behind. You must see that, coming from France.'

'Most women in France deliver in hospital, Charlotte, with a midwife in attendance.'

'But it is the home of Odent.' She couldn't believe what she was hearing.

'*Oui*, but it is not embraced by the country as a whole.'

'But women need choice, Xavier.' She heard her voice rise and she breathed in deeply. 'Sorry, I will get off my soap box but I feel very strongly about this.'

'I can see that.' His dark eyes sparkled and she glimpsed a sense of humour. She remembered his quip on the phone earlier.

'It is important to have passion, Charlotte.'

His warm smile softened his cheekbones, giving him a totally different look. A look that turned her insides into a quivering mess. A look she longed to see again.

'But passion isn't enough.' His tone, still soft yet lined with steel, instantly grounded her thoughts. 'It's a tough world and if we want to compete we have to be fiscally responsible. This programme is very small so it is likely to be costing money rather than saving it.' Xavier flicked the map over as if to say, 'subject closed.'

Charlie bit her lip and focused on the road. She wanted to scream, she wanted to rant, 'It's not fair!' But when was life ever fair? She knew she had a battle on her hands.

A battle to save her programme.

A battle to keep her irrational attraction for this man under control.

CHAPTER FOUR

CHARLIE pulled up to the McAllisters' gate, the engine idling. Xavier immediately jumped out of the car and walked toward the gatepost. The headlights picked up the way the fabric of his shorts stretched over the curve of his behind as he moved to unhook the chain.

A flush of tingling raced through her. She should *not* be noticing things like that about him. He was her boss.

Yellow light from the house spilled down the long drive and David walked out to meet them.

'How's Julie?' Charlie called over her shoulder as she started to unload equipment.

'She's still organising me, so I know it's early days yet.' David laughed. 'At least the kids are sound asleep so it's been really great having an uninterrupted conversation, even if it is the middle of the night.'

'It's good you can see the positive at this time of night.' Charlie smiled. 'David, I'd like you to meet Dr Xavier Laurent. Julie met him at clinic last week.'

David extended his hand. 'G'day. Jules said you're from the Côte d'Azur. Welcome to our farm.'

'Thank you for having me here.' Xavier returned the handshake.

Charlie's palm tingled in memory of the first time he'd shaken her hand. Cross with herself for letting the memory intrude, she vigorously pulled at the portable oxygen cylinder. It shot forward, teetering on the edge of the cargo area. Attempting to break its fall, she jammed it in place with her hip, ignoring the pain that signalled a bruise was on its way.

'Got it.' Xavier suddenly appeared beside her, his hands underneath the cylinder, taking the weight.

Heat rushed to her face, embarrassment tagging her. 'Thank you.'

'Je vous en prie.' His eyes danced with reflected light. 'You are most welcome.'

Slow heat glowed inside her. *Stop it!*

So the man spoke with a rich, glorious accent that made her feel like her blood had melted into a river of velvety smooth chocolate. So what? She had a baby to deliver.

She flung her medical bag up high on her shoulder and walked inside ahead of the men, who stood on the veranda, discussing the price of beef. Charlie found Julie walking around the kitchen.

The very pregnant woman gave her a wave. 'I've been walking since David rang you. My contractions are pretty weak and irregular, so I'm trying to get them going.'

'Let's have a look at you, then.' Charlie followed Julie to her bedroom. She wrapped the blood-pressure cuff around her arm. 'I'll do a set of baseline observations and listen to the baby's heartbeat.'

Julie settled down against her pillows. 'Funny how the last two were such quick labours and this one feels different.'

Charlie nodded. 'Third babies often do this. Part of it might be you knowing this is your last pregnancy, and you don't want to give the baby up just yet.'

Julie rubbed her lower back and grimaced. 'Believe me, I'm ready to hold this one in my arms.'

She smiled. 'Well, your BP is fine. Now, let's just see how this baby is lying.'

Julie lifted her nightie and Charlie palpated her stomach, feeling the lie of the baby. 'Great, we have a head down here and a bottom up there.'

She laid Julie's hand on the baby's bottom. 'This baby is slightly posterior, which is why your back is aching and why the contractions are a bit hit and miss.' She laid her ear against the black trumpet of the Pinard stethoscope, counting the baby's heartbeats.

She straightened up. 'And that's a textbook heart rate as well. So if you just keep walking, we can try and get these contractions a bit more regular.'

'Back to walking, then.' Julie struggled up and walked to the bedroom door. 'Hopefully David and Xavier have brewed a pot of tea.'

Charlie followed Julie into the lounge room and sat down on the couch. 'I'll just write down the obs and then I'll join you.'

'OK.' Julie waddled toward the kitchen.

Charlie entered the details of the observations and the palpation into Julie's medical history.

'Everything OK?'

She jumped in surprise, her pen scrawling across the page. She licked her lips, steadying her breathing. 'Fine. Everything is fine.'

Xavier looked over her shoulder as she finished the entry. 'Her contractions are irregular, *oui*?'

'They are.' The warmth of his breath stroked the back of her neck. She gripped her pen firmly and kept writing.

'Why are you here so early?' Xavier sat down next to her, the old couch cushions giving way under his weight and tilting her toward him.

She braced herself so she didn't fall against his broad shoulder. 'The last two labours were precipitate. Harry came in three hours and twenty minutes and Bonnie was two hours. That's one of the reasons Julie wanted a home birth. She didn't want to face going through transition in David's ute again.'

Xavier laughed. 'If the ute is the vehicle we parked next to then I certainly cannot blame her for not wanting to drive into town in that. I doubt it has many springs left.' He stood up. 'So what do we do now?'

Charlie glanced up at him, seeing a mixture of eager anticipation for the job ahead and frustration at the current impasse. He'd be more used to inducing labour rather than waiting for nature to take its course.

But to give him credit, he was trying hard to stay in the background, letting her do her job and truly observe her at work. For the first time she sensed companionable co-operation. A vital step toward saving her programme.

'Charlie!' Julie's voice hailed her from the kitchen.

Charlie hauled herself up from the depths of the soft couch and smiled at Xavier. 'I think you just got your answer.'

They found Julie with her nightie up around her waist, standing in a large puddle of amniotic fluid. David stood holding a mop.

'I don't understand.' Julie's brow furrowed in confusion. 'My waters broke a couple of hours ago so what's this?'

'You must have had what we call a hind water leak. That can happen when the baby is not quite in the right position. Then, when he or she moves into place, the main part of the sac breaks and, whoosh.' Charlie grinned. 'I think you might find things speed up a bit now.'

And as if on cue, Julie's face contorted. She gripped the kitchen bench as a contraction hit her. 'Oh, I remember this.'

Charlie checked her watch to time it. 'Sixty seconds and strong. You're on your way.'

'I want to get into the shower.' Julie headed into the newly renovated bathroom, which had a double shower.

Xavier stepped forward, pushing a large red exercise ball. 'You might feel more comfortable sitting on this, rather than standing.'

Amazement spun through Charlie. She hadn't expected Xavier to think of the ball.

Julie sank down gratefully, resting her back against the wall of the shower. David held the hand shower attachment, gently spraying warm water on her back.

Silently they evolved into a team. Charlie kept a close monitoring eye on both mother and baby, while the men kept Julie comfortable.

'I will get some cool water for her.' Xavier stepped out toward the kitchen.

'Thanks.' She hadn't expected him to take on such a hands-on role as part of his supervision. Yet he'd blended in seamlessly, anticipating everyone's needs. It was like they'd worked together as a team for a long time.

Somehow he'd managed to be involved but in a low-key way, completely respecting the wishes of the McAllisters. He whipped between the kitchen and the bathroom, keeping Julie supplied with ice and cold water.

'Please, drink. We do not want you dehydrated.' He held the sports bottle to Julie's lips, an encouraging smile clinging to his lips.

Charlie shook her head in disbelief. She'd never seen an obstetrician behaving as a doula before but Xavier was giving it a good shot.

'I'm cold.' Julie pointed to her stomach. 'Water, here.'

Charlie draped a blanket across Julie's shoulders to keep her warm and David moved the shower nozzle to spray on Julie's tummy. Julie didn't speak, her focus now firmly on her working body and her baby.

It was a great sign. One every midwife liked to see.

The heat of the shower, combined with the heating light and the warm night, turned the bathroom into a humid tropical oasis. As Charlie stood up from listening to the foetal heart, silver spots danced in front of her eyes. 'I'll just grab a glass of water, David, and I'll be right back.'

She stepped out into the hall, pulling her hair back off her neck, twirling it up onto the top of her head. She leaned back against the wall, letting the breeze from the ceiling fan deliciously cool her overly hot skin.

'Are you all right?' Xavier's voice sounded husky and worried. 'You look flushed. Here, drink this.' He pushed a glass of iced water toward her.

Charlie took the water gratefully. 'Thanks. I don't think it will be long now. She's been in transition for the last few contractions.'

'You need to look after yourself, Charlotte.' His concerned tone mixed with a gentle reprimand. 'You are no use to your patient if you faint.'

A prickle of indignation started to form at his criticism. She was a professional, she knew what she was doing, she—

The inner voice interrupted. *He's got a point. You know you push yourself too much.*

'Aagh!' A low guttural moan came from the bathroom.

Charlie and Xavier raced back in.

'I…think…I…want…to…push.' Julie rose up from the ball.

David steadied her. 'Do you want to move, love?'

Julie dropped her head against his shoulder. 'I don't think I can.'

David braced his back against the shower wall while Julie put her arms around his neck. As the next contraction hit her she dropped into a supported squat position.

Xavier handed Charlie a pair of gloves and she was struck by the role reversal.

'Push when you want to and I'll have a peek.' Charlie put her gloves on and knelt on the shower floor.

'Aagh!' Julie pushed.

'Fantastic! I can see a patch of black hair.' She shifted slightly. 'Pant, Julie, pant. You don't want to blast this baby out into the world. Just breathe her out gently.'

Slowly the baby's head crowned and was born. 'Just checking for cord.' She inserted her finger between the baby's head and the vaginal wall, carefully easing a loose loop over the baby's head.

'You're doing so well, Julie. With the next contraction I want you to push gently and I'll deliver the shoulders.'

Julie nodded, her full concentration centred on the contraction.

The next moment the baby slithered out into Charlie's waiting hands. A lusty cry filled the air.

She caught Xavier's glance of pure delight. Something akin to pleasurable pain flared and just as quickly burned out, leaving a small empty space. For a brief moment bewilderment hovered and then the surge of familiar emotion cascaded over her.

She blinked furiously to avoid a tear rolling down her

cheek. No matter how many babies she delivered, the emotion of the event affected her every time. She passed the baby up between Julie's legs into the arms of her mother, staying silent about the sex.

'Oh, David,' Julie's voice caught. 'It's Madeline.' Julie's body trembled and she leaned hard against David for support.

David nodded toward Xavier. 'Mate, can you hold Maddie for a minute while I hold Jules?'

'My pleasure.' Xavier stepped forward with a warm bunny rug while Charlie clamped and cut the cord. Xavier quickly dried Maddie and expertly wrapped her up in a baby bundle, his quick and dexterous actions infused with gentleness.

Julie squatted down and delivered the placenta, which came out quickly and intact. Supported by Charlie, she walked the few steps to her bedroom and settled back onto a triangular pillow. With a look of wonder she reached out for Madeline. Then, with the baby firmly in her arms, she gazed at her, counting her fingers and toes.

David lay down next to her, placing his pinkie inside Madeline's palm, which she gripped firmly. His gaze whipped between Julie and Madeline, love and joy etched clearly on his face.

Charlie glanced at Xavier. He caught her look. A thread of understanding wove between them. Together they quietly left the room so the parents could get to know their new daughter.

Xavier broke the silence as they reached the kitchen. 'Celebratory cup of coffee, Charlotte?'

She smiled at him. 'I'd love it.'

When the coffee was brewed and the milk warmed, they walked out onto the veranda into the freshness of a new dawn.

Across the paddocks the first rays of sunlight caressed the browned summer grass. The promise of another hot day.

Leaning against a veranda post, Charlie hugged her mug of coffee, her body tingling with awareness as Xavier walked across the veranda boards. Her body had developed a radar, telling her exactly where he was in a room at any given moment. A radar that both thrilled and exhausted her.

He stood next to her, leaning forward, his strong forearms resting against the railing as he stared out across the paddocks. 'There is something special about a new life and a new day. It is as if you have a few moments of tranquillity to savour it all before the rigours of the day demand your attention.'

His melodic voice evoked a swirl of yearning inside her. That was *exactly* how she felt.

She stared at him. His once ironed shirt was now crumpled, a lock of raven hair fell forward onto his face and the lines around his eyes betrayed his tiredness. But his eyes sparkled with the absolute joy of bringing a new life into the world— the same feelings of fulfilment she experienced every time she did a delivery.

He pushed up off the railing and turned toward her, closing the gap between them. 'You did a wonderful delivery, Charlotte.'

'Thank you.' She breathed the words out as the now familiar rush of heat unfurled inside her.

He reached out and tucked an errant strand of hair behind her ear. 'I am glad I could be part of it. Thank you.'

His touch was almost perfunctory, the 'neat gene' needing to tidy up.

A strand of hair twined gently around his finger. Instantly, the touch changed.

The tips of his fingers skimmed her skin, their feather-soft caress generating wave upon wave of sweet sensation deep down inside her.

The moment extended, strung out between them, an invisible force keeping them in place. A force keeping his finger against her temple. Keeping her temple resting against his finger. Pulling them together.

She swallowed hard, her breath stalling in her chest.

A low groan escaped his lips, washing over them both.

Their gazes connected. His eyes, now wide and darker than ever before, swirled with a fire she'd not seen before. It called to her. She swayed toward him as if in slow motion, every moment heightened with crystal clarity.

Suddenly shutters slammed down, extinguishing the fire.

The moment broke. He dropped his hand and stepped back briskly, creating a large space between them.

'Can you do the final set of observations on Julie now? I need to get back into town for rounds.'

The doctor was back. Professional distance restored.

Charlie gripped the railing, trying to steady her wildly beating heart and kick-start her stalled brain. *Think.* 'Ah, yes, of course I can. Give me ten minutes and we'll be able to go.'

She walked back inside, her thoughts a chaotic, spinning jumble in her head.

You almost kissed him.

Mortification rushed into her, burning her cheeks. How could her body betray her like that? Swaying toward him, almost begging to be kissed. She didn't do things like that. She was immune to such crazy feelings.

She loved her solo life, she was content with that.

Shivers raced through her and her body trembled, now on retreat from sensory overload. She dragged in a steadying breath. Xavier Laurent liked things ordered. He probably couldn't resist the urge to tidy up her errant hair. The man had fine-tuned 'neat and tidy' into an art form.

There's more to him than you thought. The unwelcome voice in her head boomed loud and clear.

She blew out a breath. So much had happened it was impossible to take it all in. Everything she'd thought to be true about this man had just been turned on its head.

In the early hours of the morning she'd seen a new side to Xavier. She'd met the caring doctor, not the number-cruncher. He'd been respectful of the McAllisters, he'd been respectful of her and her role. He'd even complimented her on her delivery.

He completely perplexed her.

Part of her didn't want to acknowledge this new side of him. Seeing him as the enemy made it so much easier not to like him. She didn't want to like him.

But suddenly lines were blurring. How could you fight when you *liked* the enemy?

Xavier shaved quickly. It was almost seven a.m. and he was expected at rounds. He needed to be at work. Work was safe—it had an expected rhythm, clear boundaries and expectations.

It also had a lot of people around so he wouldn't be alone with Charlotte.

Alors. What had he been thinking when he'd allowed himself the intimacy of tucking her hair behind her ear?

He hadn't been thinking at all. He'd been on such a high after the delivery, blown away by the emotional intensity that came with a couple having their baby together without the usual hospital crowd.

Charlotte had stood on the McAllisters' veranda with her

Titian hair almost on fire from the reflected rays of the rising sun, with no idea how stunning she looked. When she'd glanced up at him with her emerald eyes dancing with the joy of Madeline's birth he'd wanted to hold onto that moment of closeness for as long as possible.

But he could *not* get close to her, would not let himself get close. She was passionate about her job, which she was damn good at. She gave herself totally to her patients, which was fantastic, but it didn't leave much over for anything else.

No matter how stunning, no matter how much she heated his blood with one quick glance from her bewitching eyes, he would keep his distance. Once before he'd let desire overrule common sense. He'd paid dearly for that. He wasn't going down that road again.

The paperwork for Madeline's delivery blurred. Charlie rubbed her eyes with the back of her hand and pulled out another form. She was determined to complete all her paperwork in triplicate and have it finished early now she was being supervised.

An image of golden, muscular forearms with curling dark hairs thundered into her mind. She pushed it away by rereading the form. Xavier was working in Outpatients that morning. At least that gave her half a day's breathing space.

Half a day to find her equilibrium.

A knock on her door made her look up.

Xavier stood leaning against the doorframe, his broad shoulders filling the space.

Every nerve ending jangled. How could one man do this to her? She took in a deep breath, centring her thoughts. Suddenly, she noticed a young woman slightly behind Xavier.

'Charlotte, have you a moment?' His accent emphasised

the 'T' in her name, making it sound totally different from the way her parents pronounced it.

Swirling ribbons of sensation poured through her, delightful and dangerous. She forced out a calm voice. 'I certainly have. What do you need?'

Xavier stepped back and ushered in a woman who looked to be in her early thirties. She wore a worried expression and an air of anxiety clung to her.

'Please meet Anne Brickson.'

Charlie stood up and smiled. 'Hi, Anne. Come in and take a seat.' Was Xavier referring someone to the programme? Yes! She wanted to high-five someone in her excitement.

Anne sat down with her knees rigidly pushed together, clutching her handbag on her lap.

Charlie glanced over at Xavier and raised her brows. He nodded as if to say, Yep, she's one stressed-out woman.

'So, Anne, how can I help you today?' Charlie pulled over a chair and sat down next to her. Out of the corner of her eye she noticed Xavier sit down, too. Uncertainty flicked through her. Was this an observation session or a referral? She wished she knew, but right now she needed to concentrate on Anne and forget Xavier was there. *Yeah, right!*

Anne twisted her handkerchief in her hand. 'You see, I've been trying to get pregnant for a while now and…' Her voice started to break.

Charlie put her hand on Anne's shoulder. 'Would you like a cup of tea? It always makes me feel better when I'm a bit low.'

The woman smiled gratefully. 'Thank you. That would be lovely.'

'Xavier, what about you?' Charlie stood up, plugged in the electric kettle and set out mugs, milk and sugar.

'Tea would be lovely. Do you have Earl Grey?'

She gave him a winning smile. 'The hospital budget doesn't quite run to that, Doctor.'

A smile danced around his strong mouth. 'I thought all nurses kept a secret supply of great tea and special biscuits.'

A laugh escaped her lips. 'They do if they have time to go to the supermarket.' She glanced at Anne, whose face had relaxed into a smile.

'You two get along well.'

Surprise fizzed inside her. Did they get along well? She spent most of her time trying to second-guess him. But there had been brief moments when they'd seemed to be in sync. Like this morning, when they'd delivered Madeline.

She caught Xavier grinning at her discomfort. Fiend. She laughed. 'Sometimes we do, Anne. You're seeing us on a good day.'

She poured the tea and sat down again, directing all her attention to her client. 'So, Anne, how long have you been trying to get pregnant?'

'Matthew and I have been trying for the last year to have a baby.' Anne sighed. 'Dr Carson ran all the tests and we're both fine. He said it's just a matter of time.' She inclined her head toward Xavier. 'But Dr Laurent suggested I learn about my cycle to help things along. He suggested that you'd be the perfect person to teach me.'

Sheer delight ricocheted through her. She wanted to sing. He'd referred someone to her. He was acknowledging the programme. She sneaked a quick peek at him, but his mug of tea masked his eyes.

She flicked open a folder. 'I'd be happy to teach you natural family planning. I'd also like to give you some information on folic acid, healthy eating and exercise.'

'What's folic acid?' Anne sat forward, her interest showing in her face.

'It's one of the B-group vitamins and it's important to take it before you get pregnant. It helps prevent neural-tube defects like spina bifida.'

Charlie passed Anne a pamphlet. 'You and Matthew might like to come to one of my "early bird" classes. These are for people who are thinking about getting pregnant or who are newly pregnant.' She handed the pamphlet to Anne.

'I'll think about that. Right now I find it hard when I hear someone is pregnant because I really want to be.'

Charlie nodded. 'Yes, when we decide to have children we want it all to happen yesterday.'

'Oh, yes, that is exactly how I feel!' Anne put her hankie in her bag. 'So, how long did it take you to get pregnant?'

The question hit her out of the blue, completely distracting her. Most of her patients had been in the district longer than her and knew she was single. 'Ah, I don't have any children.'

Part of her wanted to add 'yet', but there was no point. When she'd left Richard, she'd also left that dream, too. The Buchanan women failed at relationships. Her parents' marriage had submerged her mother's happiness—her father's needs winning every time.

Richard's betrayal had driven away any doubts that she might be better at relationships than her mother. So she'd vowed to stay single and maintain her sense of self.

A seed of sadness unexpectedly turned over inside her.

She quickly squashed it. She'd chosen her life and was perfectly content.

Anne patted Charlie's arm. 'I guess you work pretty long hours, which wouldn't really suit a family.'

Indignation spurted like a geyser inside her. How dare this

woman feel sorry for her? She opened her mouth to comment but Anne continued.

'Still, Amaroo's lucky to have such a dedicated midwife, isn't that right, Doctor?' Anne beamed at Xavier.

Xavier gave a brief nod, but Charlie caught a flash of something in his eyes, which surged and fell away just as quickly. Emptiness—a type of loss?

Puzzlement mixed with indignation. She clung to indignation, the safer emotion. She didn't have to justify herself to this woman. She'd fought hard for her identity. She wasn't giving it up for anyone or anything.

Besides, she delivered babies for a living and she babysat for friends. She didn't have a childless life.

She pulled the conversation back to safer territory. 'Let's focus on these charts, shall we? I'll give you a few charts so you can record your temperature each day. Do you have a digital thermometer?'

Anne nodded and leaned in closer to the desk, looking at the mock chart with interest as Charlie explained the effect hormones had on body temperature and taught her about the biphasic chart.

'Come and see me in two weeks and bring your chart. In the meantime, if you have any questions, just ring me.'

'Thanks so much, Charlie. I can't wait to start.' Anne gathered up her papers. 'Goodbye, Doctor.'

Xavier stood up. 'Goodbye, Anne. Good luck with it all.'

The moment Anne left, he turned to Charlie. 'Come. I'll buy you a cappuccino in the cafeteria to make up for that dust you called tea.'

'If you're shouting, I won't say no.' She desperately wanted to know the real reason behind him sending Anne to see her. It might just come out in a chat over coffee.

They walked down the long corridor. 'Thanks for sending Anne to see me.'

'My pleasure. It gave me a chance to see you at work in a different way. Your skills are excellent.'

His smile of praise sent a trail of wonder through her, licking at the cold, dark places she kept walled off deep down inside her.

'Besides, I thought you would be able to see her faster than the main antenatal clinic, as your numbers are low.'

His matter-of-fact words hit like icy water, instantly dousing the wonder. Her stomach churned. She tried to focus on his praise but the thought that it was only expediency that had sent Anne to her stayed front and central.

She looked up at him, trying to read his neutral expression. This review period was so hard. Being powerless didn't sit well with her, but what else could she do?

Get some help. Why hadn't she thought of that before? She could rally the women in her programme and past patients. She could get them to write letters, send faxes, send emails and show Xavier the heart and soul of the programme. He only knew the figures. He needed to see the soul.

CHAPTER FIVE

As THEY reached the cafeteria door Charlie's pager beeped loudly. She read the display. 'It's A and E again. Twice in one week, that's odd.'

Xavier's brow creased with concern. 'Do you want me to come with you?'

'I—'

Xavier's pager sounded. 'Looks like I'm coming anyway.'

A minute later Helen greeted them, holding a patient history in her hand. 'Jacinta Gordon is in cubicle one.'

Charlie didn't recognise the name.

She turned to Xavier, to find his questioning gaze centred on her face.

'Your patient?' Their words collided, spoken at the same moment.

Helen gave a wry smile. 'Neither, actually. Although Charlie saw her briefly two years ago for an antenatal check when she passed through town. That's why I called you both.'

She pushed the history into Charlie's hands. 'All I can tell you is that Jacinta is pregnant, in labour and if the noise she is making is any indication, she's about to deliver.'

Xavier opened the door for her. 'We're getting pretty good at being a team.'

His smile washed over her in a delicious wave of warmth as she stepped through the door.

A heavily pregnant woman supported herself on all fours, swaying back and forth.

'Hello, Jacinta. I'm Charlie Buchanan, the midwife, and this is Dr Xavier Laurent.'

Jacinta moaned, 'Can't…stand…up.'

At that moment a gush of amniotic fluid flooded onto the floor.

'What number baby is this, Jacinta?' Xavier caught the latex gloves Charlie tossed at him.

She pulled a pair on herself. If this was a second pregnancy, the baby would be arriving very soon.

'Second.' Jacinta ground the words out as the contraction strengthened.

Charlie threw a ground sheet onto the floor and opened a delivery pack. She took one look at Xavier's Italian suit and wondered if he'd hand the delivery over to her. Obstetricians generally preferred their patients up on the bed, not down on the floor.

Xavier picked up a second sheet, doubled it up and dropped it onto the floor. He threw her a resigned look, knelt down next to her and whispered, 'You'll give me the name of a good dry-cleaner, won't you?'

Amazement rocked through her. He didn't fit the mould she so wanted to put him in. She kept seeing glimpses of him as a person rather than a doctor and together they built an intriguing picture.

'Seeing as you got a delivery this morning, I figure this one's mine.' His boyish grin made her heart skip.

It seemed a fair deal. Picking up the Doppler, she listened to the foetal heart. 'One hundred and twenty.'

'OK, Jacinta.' Xavier's quiet voice soothed. 'We want to guide this baby out so push when I say and pant when I say stop.'

'I'll try.' Jacinta's voice cracked as another contraction hit.

More fluid gushed. The baby's head crowned. 'Pant, Jacinta.'

A pink, bald head slowly eased its way out and then the shoulders and body slithered out quickly into Xavier's hands. His hold on the baby seemed almost reverent before he quickly handed the child to the mother, who had rolled into a sitting position.

'Fantastic effort, Jacinta. This little man wanted to come out into the world pretty quickly.'

'You're telling me!' Jacinta joked weakly.

Charlie mentally estimated the weight to be about two kilograms, which was small for a full-term baby. Instinctively, she put her hand on Jacinta's abdomen. Her fingers met Xavier's hand. Sparks of need showered through her.

She quickly withdrew her hand. 'Sorry, it's second nature to check.'

He smiled. 'It's a good habit. Go right ahead. I'll get the Syntocinon.'

She gently pressed down on Jacinta's tummy, her fingers outlining an extremely bulky uterus. Concentrating hard, she carefully used both hands and explored the abdomen. Limbs.

'Xavier,' she spoke quietly. 'I think we have a twin on board.'

He blinked in astonishment. He dropped down next to her, his long fingers dexterously palpating Jacinta's abdomen.

The action mesmerised her. An image of his fingers against her skin whizzed through her, flushing her with heat. *Stop it.*

'Jacinta, have you had any antenatal care?' His French accent seemed stronger than ever, a sure sign he was worried.

Jacinta looked up from examining her baby. 'Well, I've moved around quite a bit and...' Her voice trailed off.

Xavier frowned. 'So that is no?' His hands quickly traced the outline of the twin. His gaze met Charlie's, his eyes full of admiration. 'A good save, Charlotte.'

His words wrapped around her. She knew exactly what he meant. If they'd given the Syntocinon without detecting the twin in the uterus, they'd have risked disaster.

He stood up. 'Jacinta, you're having a second baby. I need to examine you on the bed.'

'Two?' Her face blanched white with shock and she cuddled her baby close. 'Well, this one came out OK, so the next one should be a cinch, right?'

Charlie exchanged a cautious look with Xavier as she took the baby from Jacinta.

Xavier helped the woman up onto the bed. 'The second twin can sometimes get into a difficult position. I am hoping we can deliver it without you needing a Caesarean section.'

Fear crossed Jacinta's face.

Helen popped her head through the door. 'Everything all right?'

Charlie grimaced. 'Undiagnosed twins, Helen. Please, take the baby to Special Care and ring the anaesthetist now in case we need a spinal block.'

The charge nurse started. 'Can do. What else do you need?'

'A forceps set.' Charlie's voice blended with Xavier's.

Xavier palpated Jacinta's abdomen, his hands locating the lie of the baby. 'Oblique.' He muttered the word as if it were an expletive.

Charlie closed her eyes for a moment and took a deep breath. This wasn't good for either mother or baby.

Xavier's voice belied the growing concern in his eyes.

'Jacinta, your baby is lying across your uterus. I want you to use the mask and breathe in nitrous oxide while I try and turn the baby so it is head down and ready for delivery. The more relaxed you are, the easier it will be.'

Unexpected surprise flowed through Charlie. He was going to try for a normal vaginal delivery first, even though it would be very tricky.

She handed Jacinta the clear mask.

His large hands flexed and caressed, guiding the baby's head across the brim of the pelvis. He checked the position by pressing deeply just above the symphysis pubis—Pawlik's grip.

He caught Charlie's gaze and shook his head, his frown deepening. 'Jacinta, I have to try again so breathe deeply.'

The woman's eyes dilated with fear but determination shone from her face. 'What ever you say, Doc.'

Charlie recorded the foetal heart rate. It was holding steady.

Suddenly Jacinta groaned as a strong contraction hit.

Xavier's shoulders stiffened. 'Gloves.' Urgency poured through the single word.

Charlie quickly opened the gloves, knowing Xavier needed to guide the baby's head into the pelvis without it compressing the cord and depriving the baby of oxygen.

The Doppler sounded loud in the room as she counted. Recording the foetal heart was the only tool they had to assess if the baby was coping well. Or not.

'One hundred.' Her voice sounded firm but her heart hammered at the slow heart rate. Even if they raced her to Theatre now, it might be too late.

Sweat broke out on Xavier's brow, his concentration fully on guiding the baby through the birth canal.

'Amnihook.' He steadied the twin's head over the brim of the pelvis, muttering in French.

'Will the baby be all right?' Jacinta's raw fear solidified.

'Dr Laurent is doing everything he can. You're in good hands.' Charlie spoke spontaneously, trying to reassure the woman.

Realisation poured through her. She believed every word she'd spoken. He was one hell of a doctor.

'Foetal heart again.'

She held her breath as she rubbed the Doppler over Jacinta's abdomen. A whooshing sound like horse's hooves boomed through the room. 'One twenty-five and steady.' *Yes!* He'd done it.

His eyes sought hers, smouldering relief glowing brightly from their inky depths. Something unfamiliar turned over inside her.

Xavier gently removed his hand now the baby's head was safely in the birth canal. 'You're a very lucky young woman, Jacinta. This baby is head down and in the correct position. Now we wait for the next contraction.'

They didn't have to wait long. Four pushes later a baby girl slithered into Xavier's arms.

Xavier stroked the baby's head. 'Well, young lady, you gave us a bit of a scare but you're here now.'

For a few moments the three of them quietly enjoyed the satisfaction of a disaster averted and a new life entering the world.

Stuart Mullins, the paediatrician, strode through the door. 'Got another baby, I believe?'

The next ten minutes passed quickly. The baby girl went to join her brother in Special Care Nursery and Jacinta was transferred to the postnatal ward.

Silence descended and Charlie started cleaning up the room on autopilot, her thoughts completely absorbed by the last hour's events. Xavier's technical skills had been brilliant. Amaroo was lucky to have him.

'Charlotte, do you have any plans this evening?' His low voice broke into her reverie.

Her breathing stalled. *Yes! No!* Thoughts bounced around in her head, confusing her. Was he asking her out?

She didn't want to be alone socially with him, she didn't trust herself. 'I, ah…' her stammering voice sounded completely incoherent.

He gave a wry smile. 'I am sorry, that did not come out quite right. No need for you to panic, I am not asking you out.' Irony filled his voice. 'After my experience in France I am totally separating work and pleasure.'

Curiosity chased away her panic, helping her regain composure. Did this have something to do with his comment in Theatre about the past interfering where it shouldn't? 'Why are you separating work and pleasure?' She tossed dirty linen into the skip.

His shoulders stiffened. 'It does not work.'

Bitterness clung to his words, surprising her with their intensity.

His face tightened, his olive skin taut across his cheekbones. 'Medicine means crazy hours. Two people cannot be dedicated to their career, each other and a family. It leaves no time to build a marriage, to create a real family. It is no way to run a relationship.'

The comment intrigued her. 'Run a relationship? You make it sound like a business.'

'Perhaps if people had relationship plans, like business plans, the divorce rate would be lower.' The muttered words were barely audible.

Astonishment filled her. 'I thought the French believed in passion. Are you saying you think we should be more cerebral in our choice of partners?'

He shook his head. *'Non*, passion is very important. However, you can find passion in many places. I am saying that people should look outside their own pond. Find a person who shares their dream. Right now I am not looking for a relationship at all. But if I was, I would only date outside medicine.'

He silenced any further comments by pulling out his palm pilot. 'Back to tonight. I have a full diary this week and I know you have back-to-back clinics and two imminent deliveries. I need to discuss the clinic figures with you as soon as possible. I thought perhaps we could do it out of hours when the phone will be less likely to interrupt us.'

Her heart slammed against her chest. Spending time alone with Xavier, even though it wasn't a date, wouldn't be safe for her state of mind or her heart.

But going over her programme's budget was important. She visualised her diary and breathed in deeply, forcing out a calm voice. 'Tonight would be fine. My clinic's over at six. But as Sheila Douglas is expected to go into labour any minute, it would be easier if we had the meeting at my house. That way we're ten kilometres closer to her place.'

He added the details to his palm pilot. 'As long as you let me bring dinner.'

She laughed. 'Xavier, I live twenty minutes out of Amaroo. Take-aways aren't really an option.'

His shoulders moved back and his eyes flashed indignantly. 'Let me worry about that.' His pager beeped. 'Birth Suite.' He grabbed a clean gown. 'See you at seven, Charlotte. *Au revoir.*' He turned and walked back toward the door.

Reality hit. She'd just invited him to her home! She spent more time at the hospital than at her house. She'd been so busy thinking about Sheila Douglas and logistics, she'd totally forgotten the state of her domestic life. Total chaos.

She slapped her forehead as she remembered the piles of clothes and dishes that awaited her at home.

Honestly, Charlotte, you need to be more tidy. She stomped on her mother's voice.

She wasn't trying to impress Xavier with her domesticity so what did it matter? Tonight was a business meeting and he'd only have eyes for the figures and the budget. He had a plan for everything, even down to where he should look for a future partner.

What was that all about? What on earth had happened to him in France that made him so insistent that a relationship between two colleagues wouldn't work? His words intrigued her.

She shook her head. Xavier's private life was exactly that. Private. It had nothing to do with her.

But you'd like to know more.

She checked the oxygen and suction, silencing the voice.

Xavier gave thanks for the fact it was still daylight saving time as he negotiated the rutted gravel that doubled as a road leading to Charlotte's house. He'd never have found it in the dark. An old weatherboard farmhouse with a return veranda greeted him at the end of the track. Chickens and ducks wandered about and a sprinkler dribbled out much-needed water to a parched veggie patch.

Surprise slugged him. From her timesheets he knew she spent most of her time at work, so he'd always pictured her living in Amaroo township in an apartment. Just a place to sleep. But this place declared itself a home. A haven from the world.

He stepped out of the car into a wall of heat. A squad of bush flies immediately clustered around his open-neck shirt. Grabbing his supermarket bags and laptop out of the car, he headed toward the veranda steps. He hated the fact that yet again he was extending his workday, wrangling with this budget. At least doing it over dinner made it seem less like work.

Charlotte hadn't seemed to mind. Well, not once she'd known it was a working dinner, not a social one. Her initial reaction to his invitation—a look of pure horror—had seared him. He shouldn't care about her reaction. After all, she was a colleague and colleagues didn't date. But women didn't usually recoil from him.

Her reaction puzzled him. Had a man made her wary?

He sighed, pushing the thought away. He didn't need to know. Didn't want to know. The *only* thing he needed to know was the number of enrolments and the full financial picture of the community midwifery programme. That would place him one step closer to getting the budget in line. One step closer to getting his new job under control.

As his foot hit the top veranda step, a golden Labrador belted around the corner, her paws skating on the veranda boards.

'Spanner, sit!' Charlotte, dressed in shorts and a vivid green sleeveless silk top, which matched her eyes perfectly, walked toward him, smiling.

His gaze zeroed in on her long, shapely legs that her shorts did little to conceal. His mouth dried. How did she manage to look so fresh and vibrant when she'd been up since 2 a.m.?

But as she got closer he saw the lines of weariness etched around her eyes. *Zut.* It was one thing to drive himself hard. He shouldn't be asking this much of his staff.

A self-conscious smile hovered on her cheeks and an embarrassed laugh escaped her bee-sting lips. 'I have to warn you, you're about to enter a war zone. I've been away more than I've been home lately, so we might have to dig to find the kitchen.' She extended her arms, taking one of the three grocery bags from him, her soft skin brushing against his.

A flash of heat roared through him. He steadied his breathing. 'I'm sure you exaggerate.'

He followed her into the kitchen, the wire door slamming behind him, a barrier against the flies. He glanced around. Papers, books, dishes and stray articles of clothing covered every available surface. *Chaos.* Yet at work she was the epitome of organisation.

He groaned inwardly, thinking of his immaculate and tidy kitchen at home. Clearing a swathe through the papers on the kitchen table, he put down his bags. 'You put some water on to boil and I'll make a start.'

Her jaw rose indignantly. 'It's not filthy, just untidy.' The words came out in an injured tone.

Laughter rumbled up and out, a joyful sound he realised he hadn't heard from himself in many months. 'I meant water for the pasta.'

Her tinkling laughter chimed in with his. 'Sorry. I'm a bit sensitive about the clutter.' She picked up a pile of journals. 'But I can't work the hours I do and keep this place looking perfect.'

He started peeling some hard-boiled eggs for the salad. 'Maybe you should get someone to help you with the housework.'

She shot him a long look. 'Doubling as my mother now, are you?'

'*Pardon*, I didn't mean to hit a nerve.' He fondly remembered his sister's desire to be independent and live her life her own way. His mother had smiled and supported her without criticism. But not every family connected in the same caring way. He knew he was fortunate.

Memories of crowded, noisy mealtimes in the farmhouse flitted across his mind. His family surrounded him with love, laughter, warmth and a sense of belonging. Something he had longed to re-create for his own children. But the dream had been snatched away.

He pushed the past down where it belonged and passed Charlotte a cos lettuce. 'Can you find a bowl for the salad?'

'That I can do.' She walked across to a magnificent Baltic pine sideboard, her hips gently swaying. She bent down, her shorts taut against the curve of her *derrière*.

The knife he held hit the cutting board, narrowly missing his finger. He hauled his gaze away, returning his attention to the capsicum.

She carried an expensive-looking crystal bowl to the table, balanced on top of a box of matching wineglasses and solid silver cutlery.

He watched in amazement at the quality china that continued to appear.

She caught his expression. 'Ah, the entrapments of a past life.'

A past life? He should let the comment go. He was there to eat, discuss work and leave. She was a colleague and the only things he needed to know about her was how competent she was at her job and if she was capable of making the community midwifery programme financially viable.

But from the moment he'd parked at the top of her drive he'd been intrigued by the other side of Charlotte, the side that existed outside work. As well as the china, he'd noticed antique furniture. None of it fitted with the salary of a midwife.

He salted the boiling water and added a dash of oil.

She poured mineral water into the glasses, spritzing them with lemon juice. 'You're French yet you're cooking pasta?'

'The Côte d'Azur shares a border with Italy. We eat pasta too, although not as often as the Italians. Tonight I'll combine anchovies, roasted red peppers, extra virgin olive oil and parsley and serve it with Italian gnocchi. The sauce is very Provençal.' He picked up his glass and tilted it toward her. *'Santé.'*

She smiled and raised her glass. 'Cheers.'

He glanced around. 'You have some beautiful things from your past life, Charlotte.'

For a brief moment she met his look and then her gaze slid away and focused on the Parmesan cheese and the grater.

Her silence wrapped around him, uncomfortable and cool. A forbidding silence that yelled out, *Don't go there.*

His need to know about her past life grew. Did it have anything to do with her reaction when she'd thought he'd been asking her on a date? He quickly drained the pasta, gently stirring through the roast capsicum sauce, allowing the silence between them to exist. Silence often yielded results.

Charlie surveyed the table now devoid of clutter but groaning with food. 'It looks and smells delicious. Thank you.'

'You are very welcome. It is my pleasure to cook.' He smiled, trying to relax her.

She forked her food around her plate rather than into her

mouth. Emotions flickered across her face, indecision warring with resolve.

Eventually she spoke, her voice soft, lost in memories. 'I haven't used this china, this cutlery or glassware in a very long time. It seems a lifetime ago.' She raised her gaze to his, her emerald eyes filled with shadows he'd not seen before.

'Why not?' He kept his tone light.

'My life in Amaroo is very different from my life in Melbourne. I guess it could almost be compared to the culture shock you must experience coming from France to Australia.'

'But beautiful things should be used no matter where you live. Eating with friends and family is one of life's joys.'

She stiffened and muttered something under her breath before raising her head. 'Believe me, eating with my family was never all that joyous.'

His gaze hooked hers, locking with the ghosts of her past. 'Amaroo is not your family home?'

She shook her head. 'I was city born and bred. Schooled in Melbourne, the daughter of William Buchanan.' An ironic tone filled her voice.

The name meant nothing to him but the way she spoke it told him he needed to know more. 'Should I know of your father?'

A fleeting look of disbelief swept across her face and then she laughed. 'Dad's fame crosses the nation, but of course, not to the Côte d'Azur. My father is a well-known criminal lawyer, working for Buchanan, Simons and Carter, a family law firm that goes back to 1895.'

'Ah, yes, what is called *establishment*.' He pronounced the word the French way.

She nodded. 'That's right. Establishment both in the business sense and on the social ladder. He's often in the press about his work, although more recently he's been there for his social activities.' A brittle hardness entered her voice.

'So you grew up with paparazzi?' Sympathy for her moved inside him. He would have hated to have had his childhood recorded in the public eye. Children needed to play and romp out of the glare of flashbulbs.

She shook her head. 'No, thank goodness. Although I had one very public episode which I suppose I should tell you before someone else does.'

Tell me everything. 'Only if you wish to.' He forced his words out calmly, knowing he needed to tread carefully.

She twiddled the stem of her glass. 'I was engaged to be married to a lawyer from my father's firm. The gossip magazines called it the Melbourne society wedding of the year, the joining of two prominent families.'

She tilted her jaw defiantly. 'I called the wedding off three hours before it was to take place. The magazines had a field day for the rest of the month.' Pain, resolve and relief circled each other on her beautiful face.

'No one should marry unless their heart is totally committed to the other person.'

'Oh, my heart was committed.' She gave a wry smile to cover the tremble in her voice. 'But marriage for the Buchanan family is more to do with business than family and my fiancé, Richard, appeared to agree.'

A surge of unexpected anger blasted through him at the thought of Richard.

She paused for a moment, and concentrated on eating, while composing herself. 'My father is the third generation of Buchanans to work in law. My entire life Dad tried to mould me into something I wasn't. My earliest memories are Dad talking about "taking my place in the firm".'

'And did you?' He thought of their first meeting, her passionate argument, and the way she'd convinced him to review her programme. The debating skills of a lawyer.

She sighed. 'I tried. I got as far as doing my articles. But law just isn't me. Dad refused to acknowledge that. He couldn't separate me from family tradition. Richard was part of the plan. Dad's plan.'

'But what of your mother?' The moment the words left his lips he remembered her earlier comments.

Her eyes clouded. 'At that point my mother was an empty vessel, completely drained by my father. She'd lived her life through him, there was nothing of herself left.'

He ached for her, thinking of his parents' solid marriage. 'So you left the law and your fiancé?'

She nodded. 'I finally realised I couldn't lead the life that was mapped out for me. I told Richard I was leaving law to do midwifery.' She gave a snort of a laugh. 'I was so naïve. I thought he knew the real me, understood me. But it turned out he didn't really want me as much as he wanted a partnership in the firm.'

She straightened her shoulders, sitting up higher in the chair. 'Being a midwife is an integral part of who I am. Dad doesn't get it. The life he wanted for me stifled me, so I left before I lost myself completely. I came here and the rest is history.'

Xavier flinched at the hurt that marred her face. He had a close and loving relationship with his parents. His heart burned for what she'd never had. Unconditional love, which his parents gave out in spades. He could only imagine the grief she'd experienced when her family had rejected her. 'Families are not always what we hope they will be.'

She raised her brows. 'I didn't know the French were the

masters of the understatement—you must have some Aussie blood in you after all.' A smile hovered around her lips. 'I returned all the wedding gifts but soon after I arrived a few of my relatives and parents' friends sent me what they described as "house-warming" gifts.'

She laughed. 'They couldn't imagine living in an old farmhouse without fine bone china.'

The full impact of her decision slugged him. 'That was an incredibly brave thing to do.'

'What, to try and live without china?'

He smiled at her humorous defence but he didn't want her humour to act as a barricade. 'No, to call off a huge wedding three hours before it was all to take place.'

She bit her bottom lip. 'Thank you. No one has ever called it brave before.'

For the first time he glimpsed some vulnerability in the woman who always seemed so in control and sure of herself. It took amazing strength to walk away from family. It didn't come without a legacy of loss. Maybe that's why she worked so hard.

Instinctively he reached across the table, resting his palm over her small, soft hand. The gesture of a caring colleague and friend.

The warmth of her skin dived through his own, firing his blood, tightening his groin.

Stunned, he pulled his hand back. Friendship had never sent waves of longing through him. He needed to keep his distance. They were colleagues. That was all they could be.

Charlie swung her head back, her hair falling around her face like a veil, as if she was shaking the past back where it belonged. 'Richard didn't suffer for too long, and within the year he got the quintessential society wife. She does good deeds and his career has soared, which is good for both of them.'

'And did you get what you wanted?'

For a moment a far-away look entered her eyes. She smiled an ethereal smile. 'Yes, I did. I only ever wanted to deliver babies and I get to do that every day.'

'But your job won't give you the love of a husband and family.' The words flowed out naturally, before his brain could censor them.

She stiffened slightly. 'I'm happy with my job and my patients. I'm accepted for *me*. I've only just found myself— I'm not going to get into a relationship and risk losing *me* all over again. I'm done with relationships.'

Sadness for her crept into him. A beautiful woman like this didn't deserve to be alone. 'It sounds lonely.'

Laughter gurgled up from deep within her, a rich melodic sound that warmed every part of him. 'You can't be lonely in Amaroo. I'm part of this community. I belong.'

He searched her face for any signs that her emotions and her words were at odds, but the familiar mask of competence was back. She was a woman in control who knew what she wanted.

And that was fine with him. He could handle the professional woman.

'Why don't we have coffee on the veranda?' Xavier stood up. 'I noticed you had a table out there. I'll bring the coffee out and we can discuss the budget.'

'Sounds good to me. I'll go and wipe the dust off the table.' She yawned and stretched her arms up behind her head.

His gaze travelled along the smooth alabaster skin to the hint of lace and swell of her breast. Heat exploded inside him, sending shards of desire into every corner of his body. He grabbed the coffee-plunger, his knuckles white around the black handle.

Ten minutes later he carried the coffee and financial papers outside, determined to talk figures and nail the community midwifery programme's budget. He found Charlie curled up on the veranda swing, her long, slender legs tucked underneath her.

'I hope you like strong coffee because…' As he put the tray down he realised she'd fallen asleep. The fatigue he'd noticed on arrival had finally caught up with her.

Alors. So much for the budget.

An aura of vulnerability clung to her in sleep. He thought about the story she'd told him earlier. How could a family reject their daughter? How could a *loving* parent cause so much pain?

He sighed. He'd drink his coffee and then head home. He sat down next to her, and she moved slightly, her head coming to rest on his shoulder. A scent of vanilla mixed with roses filled his nostrils as her hair caressed his face. He breathed in deeply, getting his fill of her intoxicating scent. The tightness in his shoulders and legs, a part of him for so long, drained away.

He sipped his coffee slowly and then put his cup down. He should leave. But if he moved she would wake up, be embarrassed and protest that she was fine to discuss figures. And she wasn't. She was exhausted, not that she would ever admit it.

Non. He would sit a moment longer and let her rest. He leaned into the swing, taking her weight against his chest, gently placing his arm against hers.

She worked too hard. She'd given up a lifestyle and a

family to do this job, putting her job ahead of her personal life. Or perhaps it was fear of a personal life?

What had her father and this Richard done to her? What scars had they left?

Enough for her to want to live her life partner-less.

He struggled to understand. For him, family was everything.

Instinctively he caressed her cheek. Charlotte moved against him, snuggling into his chest, filling him with contented warmth. The crickets started to sing and Spanner wandered over and lay down at his feet. For the first time in months a sense of peace entered him, slowly unwinding, spreading out in coils of relaxed ease.

This was insane. Absurd.

She didn't want a relationship. And did he? Could he ever entrust his love to a woman again? Perhaps one day, but it would *never* be to anyone from work. That much he'd learned.

So what was he doing, snuggling with her?

And liking it?

Urgency ripped through him. He needed to be anywhere but on this swing with her. He had to leave. Now.

He moved his arm away, the heat of her skin no longer soothing. Suddenly burning.

The jerky movement startled her and she woke up, her face filled with sleep-induced confusion, her eyes struggling to focus.

Words tumbled from his mouth. 'I am sorry, Charlotte, but I have to go. You are exhausted. Go to bed. I will see you tomorrow.'

Scooping up his paperwork and laptop, he strode down the veranda toward his car. Each step took him away from the lovely, but absolutely-not-what-he-was-looking-for Charlotte Buchanan.

He put one foot in front of the other, refusing to look back. But, God help him, he wanted to.

Charlie sat on the swing, stunned. Her breath came in jerky gasps. She'd fallen asleep in front of Xavier. But worse than falling asleep in front of her boss, she'd fallen asleep *on* her boss.

Her glorious dream, the one she'd been having about feeling safe, warm and cared for, had been based on reality. She'd lain in his arms. How long for, she wasn't sure, but long enough for the tendrils of belonging and sanctuary to feel so very real.

The image of his discomfort and unease descended on her. He'd been kind and understanding about her falling asleep but it had been obvious he couldn't wait to get away from her. He'd almost run down the veranda.

Having a colleague fall asleep on you wasn't exactly the stuff that dreams were made of. Especially as he'd been so adamant that he would never have a relationship with someone he worked with.

Her cheeks burned hot. What must he think? How could she face him again?

Spanner licked her hand. She ruffled her ears. 'Oh, Span, I'm in a mess again. The off-duty doctor is completely gorgeous, caring and understanding. How the hell am I going to deal with that?'

She stood up slowly and looked out across the paddocks toward town. Amaroo was her sanctuary. A much safer one than a tall raven-haired doctor who set her pulse racing every time he came near.

She pulled in some air in a deep breath. Time to centre herself again. From now on she would only see Xavier during working hours. She could resist the number-crunching, budget-controlling, neat-freak doctor she saw at work. It was the off-duty Xavier who completely undid her.

Work would protect her. But she needed a job for that. She straightened her shoulders and headed inside. Flicking on the computer, she emailed past and present clients, asking for their support for the programme.

CHAPTER SIX

'Bonjour, Jane. How are you this morning?' Xavier neared the end of his postnatal rounds. 'Are you and Master Jack ready to head home?' He caressed the top of the baby's head, marvelling at how neatly it fitted into the palm of his hand.

'Just about ready, Doctor. Jack's got a bit of a sticky cord.'

Xavier pulled the nappy clear of the cord and took a peek. 'Make sure you clean it with a cotton bud twice a day, using some saline, and fold the nappy down so it doesn't rub on it.'

He washed his hands. 'In fact, let the little one have a kick without a nappy for half an hour. Some fresh air will help clean it up.'

Jane looked relieved. 'Thanks, Doctor. Sister Jamieson has made an appointment for me to see you in six weeks.'

'Good. I will see you then. Meanwhile, enjoy this little man.'

Humming, he left the ward and turned toward his office. He loved seeing new families head home to start their lives. He loved getting that last 'goodbye' cuddle and breathing in that 'new baby' smell of fresh soap and breast milk. It sure beat battling with the budget.

'Bonjour, Dorothy,' Xavier greeted his secretary. 'Looks like another hot day.'

'Indeed it does, Doctor. Warm days and warm nights. I'm looking forward to a cool change coming soon so I can sleep again.'

Xavier recalled how he'd tossed and turned last night, tangling his normally cool cotton sheets into a long, tight rope. He couldn't blame the summer heat. His restlessness had lain in dreams filled with alabaster skin, long, long legs and sparkling eyes.

He couldn't fathom his reaction to Charlotte. He didn't want to lust after her. These feelings were completely unwanted. Totally confusing.

He might not be able to control his dreams but he could certainly control his daytime thoughts. Today would be a Charlotte-free day. He needed some space.

'Any correspondence?' Xavier rested his briefcase on the edge of his secretary's desk.

'Quite a bit today, Doctor. The letters are on your desk and you need to check your emails. About fifty emails came in, all regarding the community midwifery programme.'

'Fifty? Mostly responses from the health department I imagine.' Xavier turned to go into his office.

'Actually, they're from community members.' Dorothy smiled. 'It seems that Amaroo is well versed in the latest technology. Text messages are building up on the phone as well.'

He paused and turned back to Dorothy. 'Community members?'

'Yes, Doctor. Women who have all been part of the community midwifery project.' She gave him a sympathetic look. 'I also have twenty-five phone messages and six requests for appointments, including a request for an interview by the local radio station.' Dorothy handed him a sheaf of papers.

Xavier's stomach dropped. 'Are these all about the community midwifery programme as well?'

'Yes, Doctor, they are. I'll make you some coffee. I think you're going to need it.'

Xavier walked into his office, punched the button on his computer and sank down into his chair. Usually the plush leather gave him pleasure but not today. Had Charlotte turned an internal budget issue into a political hot potato?

He scanned the emails, all from women who had been cared for in pregnancy and labour by Charlotte, all extolling the virtues of the programme. The phone messages reflected similar sentiments.

He punched his intercom button. 'Dorothy, find Charlotte and request her to come to my office immediately.'

'Alors!' He pushed his seat back and jumped to his feet, his frustration rising. He didn't need this. He had a budget to balance and he had to provide comprehensive health care to Amaroo. And that couldn't happen without some changes. The community couldn't afford to lose their hospital.

This was supposed to have been a straightforward process.

The intercom buzzed and Dorothy's voice crackled through the speaker. 'Ms Buchanan to see you.'

Xavier strode to the door and whipped it open, resisting the urge to pull Charlie in by the wrists. 'I'm glad you were able to come over so quickly.' His clipped tone barely held his frustration in check.

'Is something wrong?' Concern hung heavy on the words. Her eyes scanned his face, searching for clues, while her teeth worried her bottom lip.

The vulnerable action derailed him. His chest tightened, air shuddered into his lungs. He fought the urge to haul her into his arms and bury his face in her hair.

He struggled for control, reminding himself he was furious with her. 'Sit down, please.'

Confusion lined her face but she sat, never taking her eyes away from his.

He seated himself behind his desk, needing the barrier between them. 'Have you started an action group to save community midwifery?' The words cut through the silence.

'Pardon?'

'An action group—you know, people who rally and rage against what they see as injustice.'

She straightened her shoulders, an almost defiant movement. 'I *know* what an action group is. No, I haven't organised an action group. Why?'

He picked up the sheaf of papers and waved them. 'Then can you explain why my email box is jammed, why the phone rings constantly and why the KROO breakfast announcer wants to interview me about the petition to keep the community midwifery programme operating?'

'A petition—really?' She relaxed slightly and smiled at him, as if he were a confused child. 'I guess it's because people care. Women care. Rural people constantly have to fight for services and they're strongly attached to their hospital.'

He clenched his fingers into a fist. 'I am attached to this hospital, too. I am trying to save it.' He thumped the papers back down on the desk.

Charlie started in her seat. She laced her hands. 'Xavier, if people feel they're about to lose something, they fight. The French have a great history of protest—this is surely nothing new to you.' She crossed her legs. 'I sent a few emails. It looks like things have gained a bit of momentum.'

'A bit of momentum!' He riffled through the papers. 'There

is a petition to the minister and press releases.' He pushed them toward her. 'Charlotte, I have directives from higher up to pull the budget into line. I have to live in this community too, and you casting me as the bad guy is not helping.'

A brief look of contrition flared, quickly followed by determination. She folded her arms across her chest. 'I have *not* cast you as the bad guy. You're doing a good job of that on your own.'

Her temper hit him full in the chest.

Unfair. He'd inherited this financial problem and the baggage that went with it. He spoke through gritted teeth. 'You know the hospital debt has to be dealt with, Charlotte. You are sticking your head in the sand if you think otherwise.'

She leaned forward. 'I'm doing everything I can to show you women need this programme. I asked ten women to write to you so you could hear the stories behind the programme and move beyond the numbers. Granted, it seems to have got out of hand but I'm not going to apologise for that because it proves what I have been saying all along. This programme is needed.'

She sat in front of him, so convinced of her programme. *I only ever wanted to deliver babies.* Her words from last night boomed in his head, merging with the sting of her words about him being the bad guy.

Anger steamed inside him and words poured out of him uncensored. 'Is this programme needed by the community or needed by you? Have you ever considered that this job is sheltering you from living your life to the full? From taking emotional risks?'

Her face drained of colour—white on white.

Regret poured through him. He'd had no right to say what he had.

She stood up. 'Xavier, I'm sorry you're having a bad day,

but don't take it out on me.' She turned abruptly and walked toward the door.

'Charlotte, please, wait.'

She didn't turn, but strode out of his office, her back ramrod stiff. The door slammed closed behind her.

He hurled a French invective into the silence. Over the years he'd learned to keep his Mediterranean temper in check, especially out of Europe. Australians didn't understand the spark and the regret.

But Charlotte had pushed every button, she had crossed the line, she...

Has got you completely bamboozled.

He spun around and stared out at the shimmering ocean, his thoughts in turmoil. She frustrated him, intrigued him, filled his thoughts, sparked his professional admiration and fired his blood.

She made his emotions swing from complete exasperation to a deep longing. And that bit of insight didn't help him at all.

He ran his hand through his hair. The *only* thing he did know was that right now he owed Charlotte an apology.

Charlie vigorously tugged at the weeds in her vegetable patch, ignoring the scorching heat of the afternoon sun. As she pulled each weed out from the dark earth she pictured a black-haired, black-eyed doctor who'd caused her more turmoil in two short weeks than anyone she could remember.

She loved her work. Women deserved her programme. She hated the idea that everything she'd worked so hard to achieve could just vaporise.

She flung a weed into the bin. Then another. And another. But the physical satisfaction quickly waned. Her conscience pricked her.

She'd lost her temper, which wasn't like her. But the man generated such a surge of different emotions inside her that she'd spoken before she'd thought. Still, that was no excuse. She needed to apologise for calling him a bad guy.

She pushed her hands into the soil, the pain of his words coming back. Was her job sheltering her from living her life? Could he be right? Was she hiding behind work?

She rested back on her heels. No! She loved her job immensely. She enjoyed the acceptance she got from the Amaroo community. But that didn't mean she was *hiding* behind her job.

His words meant nothing. They were just a response to her hurtful words. He'd fired back—who wouldn't?

Except his words kept beating in her head like a slow drum and her answer didn't seem quite so convincing any more.

She squished the unsettling thoughts back down where they belonged. Life was what you made of it. She hadn't found it a hardship to fill her life with a job she loved. It was a heck of a lot easier than relationships.

She loved her independent Amaroo life. Just because Xavier had arrived—tall, dark, and handsome with a voice that sent shimmers of liquid heat radiating through her—it was no reason to start rethinking her life.

She'd created a full life here. A gorgeous Frenchman, who filled her dreams, didn't change a thing.

Enough. She planned to enjoy the pleasures of a quiet, country afternoon. Tomorrow, and apologising to Xavier would come soon enough.

Grabbing the hose, she turned on the water and sprinkled the cottage garden. Serenity trickled through her. She always found watering the garden soothing. The ducks waddled over, quacking enthusiastically at the sight of the cool, clear water.

Spanner raced around, trying to round them up. Charlie delighted in squirting them all with water, the cacophony of noise enveloping her.

'Charlotte?'

Startled, she turned with the hose in her hand. Shock rooted her to the spot. Xavier. Why? How? She hadn't heard his car.

'Charlotte!' He hopped up and down, trying to dodge the water that cascaded from the hose straight at him.

She swung the hose to the side.

He stood in front of her completely soaked—his Armani shirt clinging to his broad chest, outlining every muscle, every sinew.

Her stomach flipped, lust fired every nerve ending into a tingling whirl. 'Sorry.' The word sounded strangled and hoarse. 'You gave me a fright and I didn't expect…'

She watched, fascinated, as his hands pulled at his damp shirt. The neat-freak doctor who was always so well presented looked bedraggled and out of place.

She started to laugh. It bubbled up from deep inside her and no matter how she tried to stop it, the laughter rang out loud and clear.

'What's so funny?' Xavier fumed, looking like a fretful little boy who hadn't got his own way. 'I came up here to apologise to you and before I can get a word out you soak me.'

Charlie sucked in her lips to try to stop her laughter. 'Lighten up, Xavier. I've just found a second calling for you. You should consider entering a wet T-shirt competition.'

He took a step toward her, his eyes darkening into polished onyx. 'Is that so?'

'Yep, you might come in third or fourth.' She giggled at her own joke.

'Really? And how about you, Charlotte?' His rich voice

sent sweet sensations tingling through her. 'Where would you place?'

Her mind blanked. The world stilled.

He closed the gap between them, holding her gaze. 'Got you!' In an instant he'd grabbed her wrist and wrestled control of the hose, sending the spray back over her.

'Low blow! This is war.' Laughing, Charlie half turned, reaching for the hose, but he changed hands over her head, encircling her with his arms. She reached up to pull his arms down in an attempt to get the hose back, her palm circling corded muscle.

His laughter joined hers, a deep-timbred laugh that resonated through her. 'What a shame you can't reach it.'

Never able to resist a dare, Charlie took a lunge at the hose, knocking them both off balance. The sodden garden under her feet gave no resistance and she tumbled backwards.

Gripping Xavier's forearms, trying to steady herself, she brought him down with her into the muddy garden.

She opened her eyes to see his mud-splattered face leaning over her.

'Are you OK?' He spoke softly, concern filling his voice.

'Yes.' The word came out on a breath.

He moved slightly closer. 'I'm sorry I upset you this morning. I was out of line. In my anger I thought you'd been politically agitating to cause me grief. Which, of course, you had not. I lashed out at you and I'm really sorry.'

His breath caressed her cheek, his closeness surrounding her like a cloak. Warm. Comforting. 'I'm sorry, too. I shouldn't have called you the bad guy. We both said things we shouldn't.'

'We did, *chérie*.' His finger ran down her cheek.

'Yes.' Her heart hammered wildly against her chest.

His mouth came down gently onto her lips, a soft grazing kiss, a slight hesitation, almost a question.

She answered the question with a kiss of her own, running the tip of her tongue along his lips, exploring the unexpected softness, savouring his taste.

The noise of the ducks and the dog faded into the background. Nothing existed but the singing sensation of his lips under her tongue. Gentle warmth glowed deep inside her, fanning out and rolling languidly through her veins. She wanted the sanctuary of his arms again.

She wanted this kiss.

She ran her hands up into his wet hair, her fingers exploring, massaging and memorising the contours of his head, pulling him closer to her.

Xavier groaned, deepening the kiss, his tongue probing and thrusting, exploring, demanding, coaxing and giving.

The heat of his body fanned her languid warmth, igniting it into a raging fire. Desire thundered through her, stunning her with its intensity. She matched his kiss, thrust for thrust, wanting to explore him, feel him, touch him, absorb a part of him into herself.

His hand found her breast, his thumb grazing her nipple. She shuddered as waves of longing crashed through her, releasing the cap she'd forced down on her emotions long ago.

Hot, hungry need exploded inside her. She wanted him so much. She wanted his caring, his safe arms and his hot, demanding kisses.

She arched against him, willing him to extend his touch, to explore her body as she explored his. She pulled at his shirt and ran her hands along the length of his back, feeling his muscles taut under her fingers.

'Waah-waah-waah.'

The noise sliced into her haze of desire like a knife. She pulled backed. Cool air rushed into the space between them. 'Listen! Is that a baby crying?'

Xavier raised himself on his elbows, straining to hear.

The cry sounded again.

'I think it is.' Xavier's hoarse voice rang with disbelief. 'Where's the cry coming from?' He pulled Charlie to her feet.

She scanned the home paddock but couldn't see any cars other than Xavier's. There were no signs of any other visitors. 'I'll check the four sides of the veranda and you check the shed.' She pushed him in the right direction.

She ran to the veranda, looked under chairs, in doorways, in every nook and cranny. But there was no sign of a baby.

Racing inside, she grabbed towels, picked up her emergency medical bag and headed back outside, running toward the shed.

As she reached the small structure Xavier rounded the corner, carrying a baby, his face taut with worry and disbelief. 'I found her! I thought we were going mad, hearing a baby crying out here, but someone has abandoned their baby behind your shed.'

'Thank goodness we heard her.' Charlie gently rubbed the infant, drying the amniotic fluid and some of her mother's blood from her skin, while Xavier held her in his arms. She focused on the task, suppressing the pain that surged inside her at the thought that a new life could start this way.

Xavier wrapped a second towel around the baby, hugging her close. Tenderness filled his face as he gazed down at the little girl. 'She's not an hour old and she's hungry.' He put his finger in her mouth and the baby latched on, sucking furiously.

'I bet she's cold.' Charlie reached into her bag and pulled out a thermometer. She expertly tucked it under the baby's arm. 'I hope she's not badly hypothermic. We'll know in two minutes. Let's take her inside.'

They ran to the house. As they waited for the thermometer to beep Charlie glanced at Xavier. Anger, despair and pain etched his face as he examined the baby.

'Her cord has been tied off with a shoelace. At least that happened before she was left alone.' His voice cracked. 'The mother must have felt abandoned herself. How does this happen? How do these needy people fall through our network of care?'

Charlie shared his pain and squeezed his arm. 'Often they don't feel they can come to us. Hospitals can be scary places for many people.'

She looked at the sweet face of the newborn. Conflicting emotions collided inside her. Joy at a new life. Immense sadness that a woman had gone through labour alone.

The thermometer beeped. 'She's cold, you're wet and the wet shirt won't be helping. Give her to me.' Charlie pulled off her shirt and placed the baby against her chest, wrapping a dry towel around both of them. 'Skin-to-skin contact works better than heated blankets.'

Xavier nodded. 'We need to get this little one to hospital and organise a search for her mother. She could be bleeding heavily. Who do we call from the State Emergency Service?'

'Call Helen in Emergency and she'll contact the ambulance and the SES.'

The baby snuggled against Charlie. A surge of protectiveness welled up inside her. With one small movement the baby brought to the surface all the feelings she'd pushed down deep when she'd left Richard. Leaving him had meant leaving behind the dream of a child…children.

She bit her lip and dragged her mind back to what needed

doing. She couldn't think about that now. The baby needed her care. Rummaging through her workbag, she found a disposable nappy. With trembling fingers she fastened it onto the baby's skinny bottom.

She grabbed a cotton hankie and fashioned a funny hat to trap the heat of the baby's head. Then she pulled on a baggy overshirt and buttoned it up around her and the baby.

She heard Xavier's deep voice on the phone to the hospital. The man was soaked to the skin and needed to change. Holding the baby tightly with one arm, she flung clothes out of her wardrobe with her free arm until she found an old pair of painting overalls that might fit Xavier.

He hung up the phone. 'The ambulance is coming for the baby and Helen is contacting Andrew Dennis for the search.'

'Great. Here, put these on.' She tossed the overalls to him.

'*Merci.*' He quickly hauled his wet shirt off, shucked his trousers and pulled on the overalls.

Charlie glimpsed corded muscle on taut thighs. Heat pooled inside her. She moved her gaze to the baby.

He walked over to her. 'Very fetching hat.' He ran his hand gently over the baby's head and sighed.

Her chest tightened at the caring, protective action. Xavier would make a wonderful father one day.

'Should one of us go with the baby?' If she focused on the baby then crazy stray thoughts about babies and parents couldn't take hold.

'No. We don't have a lot of daylight left. Helen is contacting Stuart so the baby will be in caring hands. We have to find her mother. Every minute counts.'

A siren pierced the air and they ran outside. The ambulance officers jumped out of the rig and Charlie met them at the steps.

'The baby seems fine, just hungry and a bit cold.' She unbuttoned the overshirt.

James Rennison took the baby from her arms. 'We'll warm her up in the isolette. Good luck with finding her mother.' He closed the doors of the vehicle and his partner drove away toward Amaroo.

Coldness invaded the space where the baby had snuggled against her. Emptiness flooded in. She was used to holding babies and handing them back to their mothers. But this was different. This time there was no mother.

Frustration jagged through her. She knew circumstances forced some women to take drastic action, but… Should she ever have a baby, she'd hold her so tightly she'd never let her go.

Xavier stepped forward, taking her hand. 'Come, Charlotte, you'll see her later. Are there any buildings on the property that the mother might be in?'

'The Purcells have a haystack about half a kilometre away. Then there's the Harris farmhouse, but generally Sue Harris is at home.' She turned around and swung her arm out. 'This direction is the beach and the caves.'

'Let's start with the haystack.' Xavier strode decisively toward the car.

Charlie grabbed her bag and followed.

He vigorously threw the gear stick into reverse and swung the car around, his face a mask of determination. The rutted track tested the suspension of the luxury vehicle. Charlie gripped the doorhandle for support.

The haystack came into view, its corrugated-iron roof shimmering from trapped summer heat. Xavier hauled on the handbrake and jumped out of the car, making straight toward the shed.

Charlie grabbed her medical bag and ran after him. As she approached the doorway she heard him calling 'Hello.'

She glanced around as her eyes adjusted to the dimness of the hay shed. Hay stood ten feet high and mice ran along the rafters. An involuntary shiver ran through her when she thought about snakes.

'I don't think she's here.' Xavier jogged back to the entrance. 'It's full of hay. There's no place to hide.'

Charlie put her hand out. 'Give me your phone. I'll ring the Harrises and ask Sue to start looking around their outbuildings.'

He passed it over to her. She checked the display as they walked outside. 'Damn, no signal. Come on, we'll walk up the hill.'

Xavier paced next to her, frustration, agitation and worry rolling off him in waves.

She put her arm on his. 'We'll find her, Xavier.'

'*Oui*, but we both know what can happen.' His voice was grim. 'She could have dropped three litres of blood by now in a post-partum haemorrhage.'

'I know but we're doing everything we can. The SES will start searching in the caves and we can join them if we draw a blank here.'

He gave an unintelligible grunt and spun on his heel, heading further up the rise.

Charlie concentrated on plugging in the numbers for Sue Harris, willing the phone to find a signal. On the third attempt it rang.

Suddenly, Xavier yelled out, pointing to a small building on the other side of the hill. 'What's that?'

Charlie turned, shielding her eyes with her hand against the blinding sun. 'It's the Harrises' pump-shed but there'd barely be enough room…'

Xavier sprinted down the hill toward the dam, his athletic stride never faltering despite loose rocks.

She bit her lip, watching him disappear around the far side of the shed. He'd gone on a wild-goose chase for sure. The pump-house barely held the pump—there would be no room for a woman. And Ron Harris would have it padlocked.

'Charlotte.' He reappeared, waving frantically. 'She's here!' He immediately disappeared from view.

Adrenaline burst through her, putting every muscle and nerve on full alert. She ran down the steep slope, her bag banging against her leg. She rounded the pump-house.

Xavier was squatting down next to a pale young teenage girl. She was backed up against the shed wall, her face lined with fear, her body language screaming that she'd bolt if she could.

'It is all right, I am a doctor.' Xavier spoke quietly with his hands loosely by his sides in a non-threatening position.

The girl looked at him, her eyes full of disbelief. She took in the paint-splattered overalls, and his mud-stained face and hair. 'You don't *look* like a doctor.'

Charlie laughed in relief and dropped down next to her. 'You're right, he doesn't. But he really is. I'm Charlie and this is Xavier. What's your name?'

The girl studied them for a moment, sizing them up. 'Jade.'

Charlie put her hand on the young girl's arm. 'We found your baby, Jade, and she's fine.'

For a brief moment the girl's shoulders slumped and her face crumpled. But then she threw her head up. 'I dunno what you're talking about.'

Xavier leaned back. 'It must be our day for finding people in sheds. The baby we found was gorgeous. A little bit cold but fit and healthy. And now we've found you, and we want to make sure you're fit and healthy, too.'

Suddenly the girl's façade fell away and she moaned, grabbing her stomach. 'I thought once I'd had the baby these pains would stop, but they haven't.' Tears brimmed and overflowed, streaming down her cheeks.

'It's OK, Jade.' Charlie gave her a hug. 'Xavier and I are here to help you. But we're going to need to examine you.'

The girl sobbed. 'Blood keeps running down my leg and I feel real dizzy.'

'Lie down on me.' Charlie guided the girl's shoulders onto her lap and at the same time checked the carotid pulse. She shook her head in concern. 'Xavier, her pulse is one hundred and two and thready. There's Syntocinon in my bag.'

Xavier frowned in concern. He snapped open the ampoule with a crack and drew it up. 'Jade, you're losing a lot of blood. This injection will stop the bleeding so we can deliver the placenta, the afterbirth.'

'No!' Jade tried to rise up off Charlie's lap.

He put his hand gently on Jade's leg. 'I know you are scared, but this little injection is nothing compared to what you have just been through. You've had a baby all on your own. This will be a tiny scratch in comparison.'

Jade nodded unwillingly, her lips compressed in a firm line.

Charlie stroked her patient's hair while Xavier expertly administered the injection via a butterfly needle into Jade's arm. 'In a minute you're going to get a big contraction and then Xavier will gently deliver the placenta.'

Jade pulled her legs up. 'Aagh-h!'

'Jade, I have to put my hand on your stomach.' Xavier applied counter-pressure to her abdomen while pulling carefully on the cord. The placenta slithered out, followed by a gush of blood.

'Well done, Jade. That was excellent.' He gave her leg a squeeze. 'You did so well with that injection, and soon you will be an expert. One more needle, OK, so we can give you some fluid so you don't feel so dizzy.'

'I s'pose.' Jade's buried her face in Charlie's lap as Xavier quickly slipped the cannula into her arm.

He stood up. 'We have to get you to hospital, Jade. How about a ride in an ambulance?'

The teenager's pale face flushed with a hint of exhausted excitement. 'Cool.'

'Charlotte, I'll ring the hospital from the hill.'

Charlie nodded and handed him the phone. 'Tell Helen we're at the Harris dam, the paramedics will know where to come.'

Jade snuggled into Charlie as they watched Xavier run up the hill. 'Coolest doctor I've ever met. I could listen to him talk all day. Kinda makes up for those daggy overalls.'

Charlie smiled. 'Yeah, he's pretty cool.' Her gaze followed him up the hill, the daggy overalls exposing broad shoulders and solid biceps.

She pulled her mind back to her patient. 'I have to check your pulse and blood pressure.' She busied herself with the observations and monitoring the drip, happy to see a rise in Jade's blood pressure.

Soon they heard the siren of the ambulance as it drove down the corrugated track. With an expertise born of experience they quickly loaded Jade into the ambulance.

Xavier started to climb into the rig and then stopped, turning back to Charlie, gently touching her arm. 'I'll go with Jade. Can you drive the car back for me?'

'Sure. I'll bring it to the hospital.'

'*Merci.*' He gave her a grin. 'Be careful of the suspension.'

The ambulance door closed on her before she could think

of a cheeky reply. She walked back to the car, the events of the evening running through her head. How did a fifteen-year-old manage to hide her pregnancy from her family? Jade was a child herself and she'd given birth to a baby. At least they were both safe and well.

Thank goodness Xavier had found her before she'd bled to death.

He'd been like a bloodhound on the trail, determined to find the baby, almost frantic. The pain on his face and his air of desperation haunted her. She hadn't expected that.

There was so much more to this man than designer clothes, a fixation on neatness and a take-charge attitude. He'd been brilliant with Jade. Most consultants had no idea how to talk to teenagers, but he'd treated her with the same respect he gave his older pregnant patients. And he'd gained her trust, which was no mean feat.

She climbed into the driver's seat. The scent of leather, mingling with citrus and soap, assaulted her senses. Xavier's scent. She breathed in deeply. The memory of his kiss replayed vividly in her mind—the touch of his lips against hers, the feel of the length of his body pressed against her, the caress of his fingers on her hot skin, creating rivers of delicious longing.

Her heart pounded faster at the thought.

She leaned her head against the steering-wheel. In one moment, one kiss had changed everything. One kiss had exacerbated her loneliness, and hinted at what was missing in her life. What *she* was missing.

One kiss had proved that she wanted to be in his arms, feel his weight against her, and have his warmth surrounding her.

But she couldn't have that.

Right now I am not looking for a relationship at all. Xavier had been crystal-clear about that. He'd even said that if he changed his mind about a relationship, it would not be with someone from work.

Why on earth was she even thinking like this? The thought of a relationship terrified her. A pain edged in under her ribs. More importantly, even if she would consider it, Xavier didn't want her.

The CD in the nursery played quietly in the corner and Xavier hummed along as he fed Jade's baby. He'd sent the nursing staff away—this was *his* time with the baby. She needed love and caring because she'd had a tough start in an even tougher world. No one deserved to be abandoned.

One of her tiny hands escaped from the bunny rug, her little fingers finding and gripping his shirt. His heart turned over, longing tugging at him so hard it hurt.

Painful memories flooded him—his child, the baby he'd never held. A life cut short before it had started. The life he'd imagined, rubble at his feet.

He pushed the thoughts away. It all belonged in the past, back in France. It was pointless revisiting it.

Australia meant a new start.

Charlotte's oval face floated across his mind. He pictured her standing in her garden, her auburn hair cascading down her back, her face alive with the joy of living. The memory of her laughter sounded in his ears.

She had tasted of sunshine and freshness, as her glorious mouth, warm and hard against his, had sent her energy flowing into him, creating a need deep inside him that he could no longer deny.

But she didn't see a partner or family in her future.

And no way was he repeating past mistakes.

So where the hell did that leave them?

CHAPTER SEVEN

CHARLIE pulled into the hospital car park, the twenty-minute journey from the farm passing quickly in the smooth ride a European luxury car offered. She parked Xavier's pride and joy, blipped the car alarm and headed toward Special Care Nursery.

She wanted—no, she needed—a cuddle with the baby. Her arms had ached with emptiness since giving the baby over to the paramedics.

Charlie reached the nursery door and pushed her palm against it. Suddenly she pulled back, the unexpected change in momentum making her sway. Her gaze zeroed in on the image through the glass. Xavier sat reclined in a rocker, crooning softly and expertly tilting the bottle as the baby sucked hungrily. The image of a father with his baby.

The ache inside her intensified. *Your job won't give you the love of a family.* Xavier's message tore through her.

Tears filled her eyes. She'd fought so hard to get away from her stifling family, to carve out an independent life so different from her mother's. And she'd achieved that. She enjoyed being her own person.

The emptiness inside her expanded. She bit her lip. Everything she believed about her life suddenly seemed hazy.

Things that had been crystal clear now blurred in a fog of bewilderment. Everything she'd clung to now seemed un-steady, ready to slip out from under her.

But knowing that just confused her more. If she didn't want a relationship, and her current life was no longer satisfying, then what did she want?

She grabbed a towel off the linen trolley and wiped her face, the remnants of the mud turning the white towel brown. Terrific. She felt emotionally wrung out and she probably looked like hell. Didn't matter, she'd come to hug a baby.

With a deep breath and years of practice she schooled her face into an impassive mask, hiding the swirling blackness that threatened to swamp her. She plastered a smile on her face and walked into the nursery, across to Xavier.

'How is she?' Charlie caressed the baby's head.

Xavier glanced up and smiled. '*Adorable.* Fit, healthy and as hungry as a horse.'

'And Jade?' She focused on keeping her voice light, while his smile made her heart beat in crazy jerks.

His brows drew together in concern. 'I'm keeping an eye on her bleeding. She might need a curette, even though the placenta looked intact. I think a bit got left behind.'

'Let's hope she won't have to go to Theatre. She wouldn't be keen on that idea.'

He shrugged. 'I think she was so scared out in the back paddock that a trip to Theatre will be a walk in the park.'

'That's true.' Charlie watched Xavier adjust the bottle so the milk filled the teat. 'You look like you know what you're doing.'

He raised his brows, his eyes sparkling. 'You sound sur-prised.'

'I am. Most blokes without kids are all fingers and thumbs.'

She looked at his shoulder, rather than risking the glorious, mind-numbing effects of his gaze. She needed to stay detached.

He smiled a wide smile. 'I am an uncle six times over. I have changed many nappies, walked the floors at night and been dribbled on more times than you can imagine.'

'Ah, an expert.' She sat down next to him and put her finger onto the baby's palm, enjoying the vice-like grip that followed. Trying to ignore the warmth that came when she thought about Xavier as an uncle.

'*Non*, it's just children and family has always been a big part of my life. I have four brothers and one sister. Our parents gave us a wonderful childhood on the farm. I remember Maman greeting us after school with mountains of food.' He sighed. 'I'd always imagined I'd be a father by now.' A wistful tone entered his voice.

Something deep inside her turned over 'So what's stopped you?' She wanted to know. Desperately.

He lifted the baby high onto his shoulder to burp her.

She waited out his silence.

'I spent two years with the wrong woman. I thought we were on the same level family-wise, that we wanted the same things out of life.' Bitterness filled his words. 'It turns out I was totally wrong.'

She wrinkled her nose in understanding, thinking about Richard and how she'd totally misread him. 'I can relate to that.'

His chiselled face hardened. 'Our future plans, it seemed, never meshed. Ambitious under-describes her. While I was busy planning our life together, she was busy planning the next step in her medical career. I was one of those steps. Once she'd achieved what she wanted, she discarded me and our unborn child.'

His pain speared her, trapping her breath in her lungs. 'Oh, God, I'm so sorry.' She reached out instinctively, touching his arm.

He raised his head and gazed into her eyes. For the first time she saw raw and naked hurt. How did a person get over such a betrayal?

He cleared his throat. 'I was so excited when she told me she was pregnant. I missed the signs that she was distracted and distant. I made excuses for her.'

She squeezed his arm, wanting to erase his hurt. 'Sometimes we just don't want to see.' She sighed remembering her own situation with her family.

His black eyes fixed on her in a long, penetrating gaze. 'You're right. I did not want to see and I did not want to look. I'd invested in my dream of a family, a future. She had invested only in herself.'

He stood, laying the now sleeping baby gently in the cot, tucking the bunny rug over her.

His actions tore at her. She hauled herself to her feet, aching for him and the loss of his dreams. All that love waiting to be bestowed on his child. A child that had been torn from him. 'So you came to Australia and to Amaroo?'

'*Oui.* Here I am.'

'With a life plan?'

He shrugged. 'No plan. I planned in France and it all exploded in my face.'

She tilted her head, needing to confront his statement. 'You told me once that you would date again, but only outside medicine. That sounds like a plan, although perhaps today when you kissed me you got confused.'

His guilty look ripped into her.

Her heart bled a little.

He stepped closer. '*Chérie*, I don't regret kissing you. There's been something between us since we met. Neither of us can deny that.' His eyes met hers, willing her to agree. 'You're a stunning, vibrant, desirable woman.'

She swayed toward him, her heart racing, a delicious bubble of joy floating through her body.

'But neither of us are ready for a relationship. And even if I was, I will not have a future with someone I work with.'

The bubble burst. Reality cascaded over her.

Creases furrowed his brow. 'It does not work. I have seen too many fail.'

She shook her head, thinking hypothetically. 'It could work, if both people really wanted it to, if both people were willing to give a little.'

Discomfort radiated from him. 'Charlotte, I'm sorry, but I'm reviewing your programme, things could change and I'm…'

Panic almost paralysed her. Embarrassment burned her cheeks. Oh, God, he thought she was talking about the two of them being a couple. Words rushed from her mouth. 'Xavier, I'm not suggesting *we* would work. Hell, I doubt we would. I just want to know where we stand after that kiss.'

He moved closer to her and every nerve ending shimmered with anticipation.

'Where do you want to stand?' He tucked loose strands of hair behind her ear. 'We are both refugees from failed relationships.' He stroked her face. 'Perhaps we are each other's transitional partner. The person who readies you for the next serious relationship.'

Her mind struggled to absorb his words, deal with what he was suggesting. 'So, you think we should have an *affair* until you find your ideal partner outside work?'

He leaned toward her, his dark hair gleaming under the warm nursery lights. 'Or until you realise you can risk loving again. Why not go with this overwhelming attraction instead of losing hours agonising over what we should do?'

Her heart missed a beat. 'You've agonised?' Wonder fanned out inside her.

His hand rested on her shoulder. 'I have lost more sleep than I can blame on the heat.'

She smiled, hugging the knowledge to herself. He wanted her as much as she wanted him.

But knowing and doing were two different things. An affair? Give into the lust, passion and desire, and to hell with the consequences? She'd never done anything like that.

Right, and what you've tried in the past really worked well—not. Trying to be someone she wasn't for Richard certainly hadn't worked. And today had shown her that shunning all relationships had only left her with an empty space inside her.

She tried to get her mind around his idea. 'So we go with the flow? Accept each other as we are?'

'Exactly. We go into it knowing it won't last for ever. And we walk away when one of us says it's time.'

His hand wound into her hair, showering her in sparks of yearning. She breathed in deeply, trying to organise her thoughts. 'We walk away, no questions asked?'

'None.'

An affair meant she could be her own person, no strings attached. His thigh rested gently against hers, his heat scorching her skin, fuelling her need to be in his arms again. *What have you got to lose?*

'Do you want this, *chérie*?' Desire blazed brightly in his eyes.

She wrapped her arms around his neck, claiming him. 'I do. But I have to tell you, this is my first affair and I have no idea what to do.'

A wicked grin streaked across his face. 'We'll have fun working it out.' He cupped her chin in his hands, his fingers stroking her cheeks. Slowly, he lowered his lips to hers, caressing them with his own, stoking the smouldering coals of her need into raging flames. Sealing their decision.

She returned his kiss, drinking him in like drought-parched soil absorbing water. Using his mouth, hot and demanding against her own, to drive away lingering doubts and fears that scuttled around the edges of her consciousness.

Her tongue explored, seeking his energy and heat, his primal need of her. Her hands flicked under the cotton gown, her fingers burning as they explored the solid muscle of his back.

She tossed her head back, her breath shortening as his mouth explored her neck, his tongue branding a trail of fire from her chin to the hollow just above her collarbone. She clung to him, her knees suddenly weak.

The jangling ring of his phone doused her in reality. She jumped back.

He ran his hand through his hair as he read the display. 'Jade is still bleeding. I will have to take her to Theatre.'

He ran his finger down her cheek. 'You need to go home, Charlotte, to your bed. But tomorrow is Saturday and I want you to pack your swimming costume and be ready at eleven. I promise you an uninterrupted kiss and a day of delights. *Au revoir.*' He dropped a kiss on the top of her head and strode out of the nursery.

Trembling, she watched him disappear down the corridor. She'd just taken a huge step into the unknown, with no map or compass. And tomorrow couldn't come quickly enough.

* * *

Xavier whistled as he drove up Charlie's rutted drive. He'd done his rounds early and had been home to collect the picnic hamper. He'd packed runny Brie, a fresh baguette, home-made olive tapenade, goat's cheese, round red tomatoes and roquette. He sighed at the lack of real French pastries but he'd packed champagne instead. Chilled and ready to go.

Phil Carson had given him directions to a quiet stretch of beach only accessible to those who knew where to find the track. He had food, he had a venue and soon he would have Charlotte.

Spanner raced to greet him as he parked.

'Hey girl, where's your owner?' He scratched the dog behind the ears.

Spanner barked in appreciation of the touch and then belted off around the house.

Xavier took the veranda steps in two leaps, anticipation of the day sizzling in his veins.

Charlie called out through an open window. 'Come in. I'll be with you in a minute.'

He pushed open the front door and stepped into a wide hall and then into the lounge room. A stack of CDs tipped rakishly on a small coffee-table. Numerous books and papers lay scattered on the window-seat and some very dead flowers wilted in a vase. His mind went back to her kitchen the other night. As gorgeous as Charlotte was, housekeeping wasn't her forte.

'Hi.' Charlie came breathlessly into the room, pulling on a shoe. 'Sorry to keep you waiting, but the phone rang just as you arrived.'

He moved toward her and took her in his arms. 'No problem. You are here now.' Her wild rose perfume enveloped him as he nuzzled her neck.

She leaned into him, her sigh of pleasure almost undoing

his resolve. But he had a plan for this seduction and it wasn't going to happen in Charlotte's untidy front room.

He stepped back, grabbing her hand. 'Come, I have a great day planned for only us.'

'Xavier.'

The tone in her voice stopped him dead. 'What?'

Contrition fluttered across her face. 'That was Jessica Leeton on the phone. She's not feeling well and I need to check in on her. Can we do it on the way to the picnic?'

Disappointment rammed him. 'Of course. Let's go.' Still holding her hand, he walked her to the car.

Charlie pulled on her seat belt. 'How's Jade?'

'She is fine. But Jade was just the start of a very long night.' He did a three-point turn and headed toward the main road.

Charlie half turned in her seat. 'What happened?'

He looked at her. Her head was tilted to one side, genuine interest and caring written on her face. Genevieve had never wanted to know about his work unless it had pertained to her.

'Erica Chambers started bleeding and we had to airlift her to Melbourne. It was touch and go there for a while. And the history retrieval system fell over. We almost had to send her without her file. The medical records temporary secretary was hopeless and could not file or find a thing.'

Charlie laughed, a warm tinkling sound, completely un-sympathetic to his woes. 'Oh, dear, an untidy temp. That would be enough to send a neat freak like you into therapy.'

'I am *not* that neat.' Indignation rolled through him.

'Oh, please.' She gave him a sly look. 'In four years I never saw the wood on Phil Carson's 0desk. You are hard-pressed not to straighten up everything you come in contact with. I'm surprised you don't ask your patients to lie straight in their beds.'

'Actually, that is not a bad idea...' Laughter bubbled up inside him, warming him, relaxing him. He wanted to touch her, lie with her, wrap himself around her. He gripped the steering-wheel. 'How much further to the Leetons'?'

'Next right.' She rested her hand on his thigh.

Heat burned into his skin. Into his blood. 'It's just a quick check-up, right?' His voice came out as a rasp.

She gave him a long, slow smile. 'Thorough but quick.'

Xavier swung the car in next to the house and five children ran out to meet them. As Charlie stepped out of the car, the two youngest children threw themselves at her legs while the older ones all started talking at once.

She scooped up the youngest, tousled the hair of the others in greeting and gave her attention to the eldest girl. 'Becky, this is Dr Laurent. He's new to town so he came along for the ride.'

Surprise filled him at the ease in which she greeted the children.

Becky gave him a shy smile. 'Mum's lying down and told us to keep a lookout for you.'

Charlie moved the toddler more comfortably onto her hip. 'Well done. Can you keep the kids occupied for another ten minutes while we examine your mum?'

'Sure.'

'Thanks, Becky.' She turned, winked and beckoned him to follow.

Heat coursed through him. He breathed deeply and walked inside.

Jessica Leeton lay on her side in a darkened room. He'd met Jessica before. She'd looked tired then and now he understood why. Five kids with a sixth on the way would exhaust anyone.

Charlie squatted down by the side of the bed and touched her patient gently on the arm. 'Jessica, how are you feeling?'

She sighed. 'Tired and a bit light-headed. It's probably the heat.' She sat up slowly and immediately noticed Xavier. 'Why are you both here?' Panic filled her voice. 'Do you think something's wrong?'

He stepped forward, giving a reassuring smile he'd found worked well with patients. 'Actually, Jessica, I came along for the ride as part of my "get to know Amaroo with a local" programme.'

Jessica smiled. 'Technically Charlie isn't a local yet, she's only been here five years.'

Charlie gave a mock huff. 'Thanks very much, Jessica!' She unwrapped the blood-pressure cuff. 'We're going to check you out and see what your blood pressure's doing. Your job is to take a few long deep breaths.'

Charlie listened intently, a small frown etching itself into her forehead as she slowly released the air out of the sphygmomanometer. 'One forty-five over ninety.'

'Is that bad?' Jessica looked anxious.

Xavier sat down next to her. 'It is not terrible, but it is not great. You can stay at home *if* you get someone in to mind the children so you can rest. And by rest I mean you only get up to use the bathroom.'

Jessica sniffed. 'I can ring Mum but she couldn't get here until tomorrow. Brad's still at the stock sales in Gheringya and he won't be back until mid-afternoon. The kids haven't had lunch and…' Tears trickled out from under her lashes.

'Jessica, it's OK.' Charlie passed her a tissue. 'Xavier and

I will look after the kids until Brad gets back, won't we?' Her eyes implored him to agree.

Xavier stifled a long groan. What could he say? *No, we can't because I have a picnic in the car and plans for a hedonistic afternoon?*

'Absolutely, Jessica. You rest and we will organise everything else. Don't worry about *les enfants.*' He grinned. 'Just to make sure they get fed, I will do the cooking.'

Jessica sank into the pillows. 'Thank you so much. Don't worry too much Doctor, the kids would survive Charlie's cooking—they've had worse.'

'Hey!' Charlie put her hands on her hips but a smile danced on her face. 'I can cook. I just don't do it often.' She tucked the bedclothes around Jessica who closed her eyes in relief.

Charlie straightened up and hooked her finger toward him, tilting her head toward the door.

Desire thudded through him. She could go from professional midwife to sultry temptress in a heartbeat.

The moment she'd stepped through into the hall, she gently closed the door behind them. 'Sorry about this.'

He tucked her hair behind her ears, running his fingers along her skin, needing to feel her softness. 'We still have this afternoon. And it's just as well I came. You'll need my help with the children.' He shot her a teasing grin.

She rolled her eyes. 'Is that so?'

'You can deliver them,' he joked, 'but what do you actually know about them once they're a month old?'

Raising her eyebrows, she smiled cheekily. 'You'd be surprised.' She walked to the back door and called the children inside.

They ran in, the back door slamming shut behind them. 'OK, guys, Mum's got to rest and while we're waiting for your dad to get home we're going to have a barbecue down by the dam. So grab your swimming costumes and towels and fishing rods.'

'Awesome!' The two older boys raced down the hall toward their room.

Charlie turned to Xavier, a sassy spark in her eyes. 'You get Jason organised. He's the two-year-old. Just rummage through his cupboards or ask Becky where his bathers and hat are.'

He laughed out loud, suddenly remembering how she could never resist a dare. He'd thrown down the gauntlet with his jibe about not knowing about children and now she was rising to it. He gave her mock salute. *'Oui, mademoiselle.'*

Jason pushed his bottom lip right out and glared at him suspiciously.

He put on his best Australian accent. 'So, mate, let's get ready for a swim.' He extended his hand down toward the child.

Jason stared at it for a moment and then slid his small hand into Xavier's palm.

Warmth and trust encapsulated in one small movement. His heart ached. He wanted a child of his own.

After a bit of a search he dressed Jason in his swimming gear, pulled a top over his head and cajoled him into his hat. Together, they walked back to the kitchen.

Bags of food covered the kitchen table. Charlie stood on a chair, raised up on tiptoe, stretching into the back of a cupboard. A smooth expanse of skin lay exposed as her shirt pulled up.

Soft, enticing, warm. His palm itched to touch it.

'Where's the tomato sauce kept?' Her question hung in the air, asked of no one in particular.

'Try the pantry or the fridge.' Xavier put Jason down on a chair and started to apply sunscreen to his face.

She stepped down from the chair. 'Why the fridge?'

'Ants. They go for the sugar in the sauce.' He grinned, fun and frivolity spinning inside him. 'Ants do not bother going into your pantry because they know there isn't much food in it.'

'Very funny.' She threw the teatowel at him, laughing. 'Not all of us can be a domestic goddess.'

But standing in that small farmhouse kitchen, she shone like a goddess. A frustratingly, unobtainable goddess. He swallowed a groan. His planned picnic lunch looked like turning into dinner. Brad Leeton had better not be late back.

'Come on, Jason.' Charlie handed him a small bag. 'You can help me load the truck.'

'No, stay him.' A pudgy finger pointed at Xavier.

She smiled straight at Xavier over the top of Jason's head, her face alive with vitality. 'You've got a fan there.' She bent down to Jason's eye level. 'Can you show Xavier where the dam is?'

The little boy puffed out his chest. 'Yes.'

'Excellent.' She straightened up and turned to Xavier. 'I'll meet you at the dam with the food and the other children. See you down there.' The screen door banged shut behind her.

Silence descended as the energy in the room faded fast. Charlie had been like a whirling tornado. Stunned, he realised that in less than thirty minutes and with a minimum of fuss she'd organised him, the children and an impromptu picnic.

Ten minutes later he and Jason arrived at the dam, Jason riding high on his shoulders.

'What took you so long?' A smile raced across Charlotte's face as she walked up to greet them.

She stood before him wearing a turquoise sarong slung

low on her hips and a bikini top of matching swirls of blue and green. Heat surged through him. His gaze skimmed every curve of her body, mesmerised by the contours of smooth skin.

She met his gaze, her eyes smoky with desire.

He swallowed hard. 'We couldn't find Jason's floaties.' How could she do this to him? How could she expect him to keep his hands to himself in front of the children while she wore clothes designed for a tropical island for two?

Time for a cold swim. 'So who's for a swim?' He swung Jason down and fitted his floaties around his skinny arms.

'Me! Me! Me, too!' A chorus of voices surrounded him.

'Come on, then.' He ran down to the water, Jason tucked under his arm. Together they swam to the middle of the dam.

A splash ball hit him on the shoulder and he turned to see Charlotte swimming over with the other children in hot pursuit. A barrage of water rained down on him.

Jason laughed with delight.

'OK, mate, time to hit them back.' Xavier handed Jason a ball.

Jason threw but it fell short.

Xavier gathered up three soggy balls and fired them back with a precise overarm throw.

Squeals of delight and indignation rent the air. Suddenly he felt arms on his back and on his legs. Becky and Sarah tried to climb onto his back while Will and Ben pushed at his legs from underwater. A combined effort to dunk him.

'You're a bit outnumbered.'

Charlotte's laughing voice met him as he came up for air.

'I can't imagine who put them up to this.' He gave her a wet grin before quickly grabbing each child and tossing him or her backwards off his shoulders.

They immediately swam back for more.

'I think you've started something.' Charlotte floated quietly on her back, watching the antics, a smile of wicked contentment firmly in place.

'My turn.' Jason kicked his short legs over to Charlie, dumping a wet ball on her face.

She laughed in surprise and rolled over, wiping her eyes.

'Jason, my friend, that is the way.' Xavier swung him around in an arc, revelling in the excited yells of joy.

Charlotte swam over, steadying herself by putting her arms on Xavier's shoulders, encircling Jason. 'You devil, Jason.' Her eyes danced with fun, sparkling in the noon sun. She dropped a kiss on Jason's wet curls.

An odd sensation wove through Xavier. A fleeting moment of tranquillity and belonging.

'Hungry.' Jason poked Xavier in the shoulder.

'It must be time for lunch.' He cupped his hand to his mouth and yelled. 'OK, lunch, everyone!'

Charlotte grinned. 'I guess that's my cue. You cook the snags and I'll butter the bread, OK?'

'Deal.'

She swam quickly to the bank, beating the children, and distributed towels as they came out of the water. As Xavier cooked the sausages he watched her with the kids—opening packets of chips to keep them going until the sausages were cooked, pouring drinks and talking to each of them.

'Who's hungry?' He put the platter of sizzling sausages down on the picnic table.

'Me!' Five voices chorused.

'Right you lot, line up.' Charlotte wrapped sausages in bread and drizzled them with sauce, handing them out as the children passed by.

For five minutes silence reigned as eating took all of the children's attention.

Jason climbed into Xavier's lap. 'Hot. You feed me.'

'OK, mate.' He held the sausage up to Jason's mouth and sauce dribbled down his arm. As he licked the sauce off he looked toward Charlotte.

Six-year-old Sarah was cuddled up next to her, and she had her arm casually slung around Becky's shoulder, leaning in toward her, listening intently to what she was saying. Since she'd promised to mind the children she'd been acting like a mother. Organised, caring, fun.

She looked like a mother.

His chest tightened. He struggled for breath. He'd spent weeks battling his feelings for this woman because he'd convinced himself he could never be with someone he worked with.

Now she sat in front of him looking like Madonna and child.

She'd taken the role of emergency babysitter in her stride, not missing a beat. Nothing fazed her. The children were relaxed and comfortable in her company, and somehow she managed to give each one her attention when they needed it.

She'd gone from midwife to mother before his eyes.

Suddenly pictures floated through his head: Charlotte in his house; Charlotte holding a red-haired baby; Charlotte in the garden, spraying children with the hose. A week ago it would have seemed ludicrous, two hours ago even, but now it seemed natural. As if the missing piece in the jigsaw of his life had been found.

She works with you. He pushed the cautioning words away, focusing instead on Charlotte.

She ran from relationships, replacing love with work. Could he convince her there was another way to live her life?

CHAPTER EIGHT

CHARLIE waved goodbye to the Leetons and ran to Xavier's car through pouring rain. Brad had finally returned from the sale yards and Jane's mother was booked on the morning train.

'Our work here is done.' Xavier planted his foot on the accelerator.

'Sorry about the picnic.' She looked at the rivulets of rain streaming down the windscreen.

'*Oui*, even the weather has conspired against me. It is time to go home.'

Disappointment rammed into her gut. Wasn't an affair supposed to be secret meetings and passionate love-making? Had he changed his mind? For the last couple of hours he'd been uncharacteristically quiet. His teasing had stopped and he seemed lost in thought. Was he regretting last night's proposal of an affair?

Please, no. She wanted this. Needed it.

Xavier passed her gate and headed back into Amaroo. 'At least at my place we can walk on the floor without stepping on anything.' He gave her a teasing grin and ran his fingers gently over the back of her hand.

His touch burned into her. She wanted his fingers exploring more than the back of her hand. 'I wasn't planning on doing a lot of walking.'

His eyes darkened. 'Glad to hear it.'

He took the corner slightly too fast and pulled into his driveway, the car's tyres crunching on the gravel. Jumping out of the car, he quickly jogged around and opened her door.

'Come on.' He grabbed her hand and together they ran through the rain to the front porch. Keeping her hand firmly in his, he pushed the key into the lock, opened the door and gently pulled her inside, out of the rain and into his arms.

She melted against him, her hands cupping his cheeks. She tilted her head, gazing at him, taking in all of him—his ink-black eyes that called to her with their unexpected shards of colour, eyes that saw into her soul. His thick black hair that curled up at the back of his neck and the lines around his eyes and mouth that merged when he smiled at her.

His arms tightened around her. She needed to be in these wondrous arms, feel them cocooning her, cherishing her, no matter how fleeting it might be.

His hands cupped her buttocks, pulling her closer to him, flooding her with his heat. A guttural groan sounded in his throat. '*Chérie*, all day I've wanted to touch you and it's driven me crazy.' He stroked her hair. 'I had a perfect seduction planned.'

Smiling at the knowledge that he wanted her, she brushed his lips with her fingers. 'Over-planning can get you into trouble.'

His eyes flashed at her teasing words, desire blazing in their depths. He plundered her mouth with his, hungrily taking what he'd waited for all day.

A fire of hot, unsated need streaked through her, overwhelming her. She met his kiss, savouring his taste, his feel, his scent. Absorbing a part of him, filling a void.

His moan rumbled deep from his soul, thudding through her veins, testifying to his need of her.

Her knees sagged as longing consumed her.

His words poured out low and gravelly. 'Plan or no plan, I am not making love to you in my hall.' Scooping her into his arms, he carried her to his bedroom, laying her gently on the bed.

He lay down next to her, his gaze fixed firmly on her face. 'You're so beautiful you're driving me crazy.'

'Really?' *I drive him crazy.* A thrill fizzed through her.

'Really.' He leaned forward, caressing her forehead with light, gentle kisses. Between kisses he spoke softly in French, his delicious accent pouring over her like fragrant massage oil.

He rained kisses along her nose, across her cheeks, down her jaw and into the hollows of her neck. Slow, deliberate kisses, imprinting his touch on her, branding her as his.

Waves upon waves of glorious sensation built, sending tendrils of aching pleasure swirling deep inside her.

His low guttural moans matched hers as he pulled frantically at the buttons on her dress, welcoming her tingling breasts as they strained against the lace of her bra.

His thumb caressed her through the lace. Rockets of white-hot need gripped her, bringing her arching against him. He deftly unclipped the bra at the front and dipped his head, his tongue rasping against her swollen nipples.

Colours exploded in her head.

'It's my turn.' The words tumbled out on a breath as she gently pushed him back onto the bed.

'*Chérie?*' His eyes widened in question.

Slowly, she raised her cotton dress above her head and let it slide languidly from her fingers onto the floor.

His gaze never left her.

Tugging at his shirt, she slid her hands underneath the soft fabric, her palms quivering as they moulded to taut muscle.

He'd used his mouth in an agonisingly tantalising way. She wanted to return the favour. Leaning forward, she undid each button on his shirt with painstaking precision, batting his hand away when he tried to help.

She gave him a sly grin. 'I know you value your clothes so I'll be careful.'

She heard him growl and she laughed, suffused with the power of giving. She turned her attention to his trousers. Her fingers brushed his erection. He groaned.

'I'll do it!' He quickly sat up, and as she moved aside he shucked his trousers.

He stood there tall, powerful and naked, the reality far surpassing her dreams. Her breath caught in her throat.

He pulled her down with him, gathering her close, stroking her, pleasuring her, driving her to the edge, wild with wanting.

She explored him, her hands desperate to feel all of him, to find places that made him gasp and hold her tighter. She committed those to memory.

He gently rolled her over and stroked her face. 'Are you sure about this?'

'Oh, yes.' She pulled his head down, kissing him hard, hard, taking her fill.

He moved over her, gently entering her, easing in, establishing a powerful rhythm.

She gasped, her breath coming in short, rapid runs. Ribbons of hot, desperate need shot through her, blasting all the way down to her toes.

She gripped his back, arching toward him, needing to feel all of him against her, all of him inside her.

Together their rhythm spiralled them up and up to the precipice, finally flinging them out into space as they shattered in unison.

She felt his ragged breathing slow, his arms wrapped tightly around her and his head nuzzled against her neck.

She snuggled in against him, his energy flowing into her, caressing her, giving her strength. She could stay here in this safe, caring cocoon for ever.

For ever.

The idea played across her mind, deliciously tempting. Tormentingly tempting. She breathed in deeply, bringing reality back into her life after half an hour of fantasy.

All this was temporary. Making love, feeling cherished, it wasn't real. She didn't do relationships. Besides, Xavier didn't want her as a life partner. He believed he couldn't love her because they worked together.

And at any moment either of them could walk away. That was the agreement.

Yesterday it had been the perfect agreement.

So why didn't it feel so perfect any more?

An hour later Charlie wrapped Xavier's thick bathrobe around her and breathed in his scent. She planned to hold the real world at bay as long as possible. She padded down the hall toward the aroma of basil and garlic.

Xavier stood in the kitchen surrounded by as much stainless steel as in a commercial kitchen. 'Hungry?' He turned from a large tureen, his smile zeroing in on her.

She smiled back, feeling deliciously warm. 'Starving. That smells great.'

'*Soupe au pistou.*'

'Yummy, vegetable soup with a sort of pesto stirred in, right?'

He started in surprise. 'You know it?'

She grinned. 'I spent a bit of time in France when I did the traditional Aussie backpack through Europe. I remember eating it at a midnight fête.'

His eyes glazed with a far away look. 'And what did you think of France?'

'I still miss those wonderful pâtisseries where you not only bought a cake but you bought an experience.' She sighed. 'None of this "shove it in a bag", like we have here. They boxed every cake, whether it be one or ten.'

He stirred the soup and sliced a baguette. 'All food is an experience in France.'

She sat down on a tall chair at the island bench and then swivelled around to look at the large open-plan living space. Unlike her antiques, his furniture was modern with clean lines. Unlike her clutter, everything was stacked neatly on shelves. The three remote controls sat lined up on top of the television.

She chuckled. 'So how many times a week do you have someone come in and tidy up?'

'I'm not going to answer that on the grounds it might incriminate me.'

His black eyes sparkled. The glow that seemed so much a part of her now, flared. 'Aha! So more than once.'

'All I am doing is helping the local economy by providing employment.'

'Yeah, right.'

'Here, eat your *soupe*.' He sat down next to her, his lips skimming hers in a brief kiss. A kiss shared by couples everywhere. One of companionship and shared jokes.

The ache under her ribs flared. *Just enjoy the moment while you have it. The future will come soon enough.*

She grated some extra Parmesan cheese. As her spoon broke the surface of the soup the aroma of the fresh herbs floated up toward her. She sipped, the flavours exploding in her mouth. 'This is wonderful.'

'*Merci.* I enjoy cooking. It helps me unwind from the stresses of the day.' A wry smile tugged at his mouth. 'Just lately, with all the budget issues, I have been doing a lot of cooking.' He sipped his soup. 'And I've been thinking about Julie McAllister.'

Charlie's fantasy collapsed around her, the real world piercing her cocoon.

Xavier broke some bread. 'She had a fantastic home birth but she could have come into Amaroo and had the same thing.'

Charlie drew in a breath to steady her for the battle she knew was ahead. 'Come on, Xavier. You were there. You experienced the difference. Hospitals and home births are poles apart. For starters there would have been more people coming in and out. Bound to have been a med student or midwife who needed to observe. And just as likely a midwife sticking her head in, looking for the drug-cupboard keys, the moment the baby was being delivered.'

'So we improve the way things are done in hospitals.' He spoke softly, his voice steady.

'No.' She heard the determination in her voice. 'We look outside the box and find a different way of operating entirely.'

He pushed his empty bowl away. 'That could be the same argument as mine.'

'Not at all. You can't "fix" something when it is based on a totally different premise. Hospitals are for sick people based on a medical model. Most pregnant women are not sick. They should be offered a choice.'

'And that choice has to be cost-effective.' He spoke quietly, the message powerful.

She rallied her thoughts. 'It can be. But sometimes passion and belief have to carry a programme until it gains enough momentum to be truly self-sufficient. Ideology has to play a part.'

His eyes sought hers. 'I am sorry but I'm not sure Amaroo has that luxury any more.'

She closed her eyes for a moment, the pit of her stomach rolling with disappointment. 'Are you saying the programme is closing?'

'*Non.* No decisions have yet been made. I just think it would be a good idea for you to think about what you might do if things change. If the programme folds, this could be an opportunity for you to try something new.'

Her mind grappled with the change of topic. What was he really saying? 'I love what I do, Xavier.'

'I know you do.' He stroked her face. 'You have a passion for your work that many people would envy but you should want more out of life than just your job. You should want more for yourself. This could be a time for you to focus on yourself.'

A wave of discomfort rippled through her. 'Don't tell me what I want, Xavier. I think you're confusing it with what *you* want. You want more than work. You want children and a family life. I'm fine with what I have.'

'Are you?' His brows rose. 'I think you have been telling yourself that story for so long that now you believe it.'

A defensive shield rose up inside her against the pain his words inflicted. 'That's ridiculous. I know relationships don't work for me.'

He reached out and touched her hand. 'Did it ever occur to you that perhaps you chose the wrong man? Or that actually your father chose the wrong man for you? Now you are denying yourself happiness because you're scared of taking a risk?' His voice dropped. 'I saw the look on your face when you cuddled Jade's baby. I saw you with the Leeton kids. I think you want a child of your own.'

His words paralysed her. She struggled to breathe against a hammering heart. With a few choice words he'd cut through everything and seen straight into her soul.

Wanting a child was one thing.

But a relationship was something else entirely.

A relationship meant risking her heart again. The idea scared her to death.

She pulled his robe more tightly around herself and forced out a laugh, trying to deflect him away from the turmoil that roiled inside her. 'Stick to obstetrics, Xavier—psychoanalysis isn't your thing.'

He pulled her gently over to him and into his arms. 'I just want you to consider this—no matter how much you want things to stay the same, change does happen. And sometimes the things we think we want aren't really what we need.'

She turned to look into his face. Care and concern etched themselves around his mouth and in his eyes. She didn't want to see that. She didn't want to be reminded that she was alone and childless. That she was falling for a man who did not want a woman like her as a wife. That her job might fold.

She didn't want to see empathy in his eyes. She wanted to see lust and desire and pretend that everything was fine. That her world wasn't changing. That her heart was safe.

She ran her hands along his face and brought his lips down onto hers, driving away reality, embracing an illusion.

* * *

'So why do we have to do this again?' Jade walked through the doors of the clinic two weeks after Ebony's birth and got straight to the point.

'Hi, Jade, how are you?' Charlie gave the teenager a smile. She found if you ignored the gruffness in Jade's voice and manner, the vulnerable young woman eventually came to the surface.

'Yeah, OK.' Jade picked up a magazine and flicked through it, not making eye contact. 'My breasts are hurting me, though.'

'Are you taking the tablets we gave you to dry up your milk?' Charlie asked gently.

Jade looked up from the magazine. 'Mostly. I forgot yesterday.'

'You need to take them for fourteen days. How about you take them when you clean your teeth in the morning? The same time you take your contraceptive Pill?'

Jade was unusually silent.

Charlie signed inwardly. 'Are you taking the Pill, Jade?'

'I keep forgetting that, too. Can't I have an injection or those rods they put in your arm?'

'Sure, if you think that will work better for you, we can make an appointment with Family Planning today. In the meantime, do you want any condoms?' Charlie opened her top drawer.

The magazine flew across the room, just missing Charlie's head. She caught it and laughed. 'OK, I was just checking! Come on, then, let's check out your tummy.' Charlie stood up and Jade followed her over to the examination couch.

Charlie gently examined Jade's breasts and palpated her abdomen. Jade's uterus had contracted well and was at the level of her symphysis pubis. 'Do you have much blood loss?'

'Nah, that's all finished.' Jade pulled up her pants and slid off the couch.

'Well, physically you're doing well. How are things at home?' Charlie tried to keep her voice casual. The physical recovery after birth was generally straightforward. The emotional recovery of giving up a baby for adoption would take a lot longer.

'Mum and Dad are still pretty dark at me. Mum is either lecturing me or ignoring me. Dad has no idea what to say so he just looks and leaves. Maybe...' Her voice trailed away.

'Your mum's still in shock. Remember you knew about the baby for six months. Mum had no idea.' Charlie cringed inside, remembering the scene Jade's mother had caused in the hospital.

'Yeah, I s'pose.' Jade twirled a scrunchie in her hand. 'The social worker says I have six weeks to make up my mind about what I want to do.'

Charlie waited, letting the silence surround them.

'I dunno what to do. I mean, I love the baby and stuff, but...' She shifted in her chair. 'Charlie, what would you do?'

'Jade, I'm not fifteen so what I would do isn't important.' Jade had been in to visit her twice this week. Ebony was now in foster-care with Sharon and Bob Jenkins, and growing like a weed.

'Bringing up a child on your own at any age is hard work, especially at fifteen with Mum and Dad not being supportive.' Charlie leaned forward, touching Jade's arm. 'Today adoption is open and you'll be able to visit Ebony and be like a big sister.'

Jade sniffed, wiping her hand across her red nose. 'Yeah, I know. I just wish it was different.' She gave Charlie a hopeful look. 'Like you and Dr Xavier could adopt her?'

'We work together, Jade. We're not a couple.' The words

slipped out before Charlie realised she'd verbalised her thoughts.

Jade sat bolt upright. 'I saw you the other day pashing in the car park at Wilson's Beach. You both looked pretty hot.'

Heat flooded Charlie's face. Discussing her affair with a fifteen-year-old wasn't something she wanted to do.

Jade continued, 'you know Dr Xavier visited Ebony every day in hospital. You're both old enough to be parents. You could talk to him about my idea, couldn't you?'

The pleading in Jade's voice pulled at her. 'Jade, I'm really sorry but we can't adopt Ebony.'

'Why not? Don't you want a baby?'

Her heart flipped. How did she explain to a teenager that life wasn't black and white? Yes, she wanted a child. But she needed a relationship before she had a child.

She and Xavier didn't have that. All they had was an electrifying affair, awesome in its own way and devastatingly lonely in another. He couldn't love her.

She'd seen his aching pain, the legacy of betrayal. He held his heart close, guarding it. Hell, she didn't blame him.

And he'd been so honest. He'd told her from the start he couldn't offer her love. He'd been so clear about what he wanted and it wasn't a midwife who worked crazy hours. And she couldn't give up what she loved, so where did that leave them?

Exactly where they were. Having an affair.

Unless… Her mind kicked up a gear, ideas pouring through her. Unless she could show him that two people from the medical profession *could* have a life together. That she was worthy of his trust and would never hurt him. That she shared his dream of a family, too.

She dragged her thoughts back to Jade. 'Yes, one day I do

want a baby. I do want to be a mother. But Social Services have a really strict system. There are families who have already been approved to adopt. Couples who have waited a long time to have a family.'

'The rules suck.' Jade slouched again.

'The rules always suck. Come on.' Charlie put her hand out and pulled Jade to her feet. 'Let's grab a hamburger before we see Mr Martin at school.'

Jade made a face and stuck out her tongue.

'If you want to do my job then you have to finish school. Besides, the programme Mr Martin has going is very different from normal school. It's more like a college.' She'd learned a few things about fifteen-year-olds in the past two weeks. 'I'll even chuck in a milkshake.'

'Chocolate?'

'Is there another flavour?'

Jade smiled, stood up and walked over to the door. 'So, you and the doc…'

Charlie almost choked. Trying to keep a straight face, she marched Jade out the door toward the car.

Xavier took a break from being a host and grabbed a glass of cold water from the hospital function room's kitchen. His inaugural hospital cocktail party was in full swing and his guests mingled outside on the hospital lawn, enjoying the warm summer evening. The flickering light from the citronella flares danced in the light breeze that blew in from the ocean.

People chatted together in groups eating the hors d'oeuvres, drinking the French pinot and generally having a good time. The only thing missing was Charlotte.

He'd been in meetings all day and hadn't been able to

catch up with her. He sighed. He wished she were here beside him with her vivacious laugh and intelligent conversation. Without her this party was no fun at all.

He gave himself a shake. It shouldn't matter if she was there or not. An affair by its nature meant occasional meetings, great sex and no commitments. They'd both agreed to that.

But that was before he'd seen her with the Leeton kids.

He sighed and put his drink down. He best get back to being host.

Suddenly warm arms snaked around his waist and a supple body pressed against his.

He spun around, catching the gaze of sparkling emerald eyes. Tender warmth flooded him. 'You're here.'

She pressed her lips against his in a brief, welcoming kiss. 'You sound surprised.'

Confusion and delight merged. 'I thought you were working.'

'I am, but it's my break. Remember, at the McAllisters', you told me I needed to take care of myself.' She grinned. 'I do listen occasionally.'

She gave him a quizzical look. 'I thought you wanted me to be here and I wanted to come.' She leant around him and popped a seafood ball into her mouth. 'Besides, I knew you'd have great food.'

'I did want you here.' He held her close, breathing in her wild rose perfume, enjoying the sensation of holding her close.

She leaned back slightly, her face serious. 'But you didn't ask me.'

'I thought I couldn't ask.'

She levelled her gaze with his. 'I worked that out.' She ran her hand down his cheek. 'When you talked about the party the other day you mentioned a few times how you needed to host it and then you mumbled something about work responsibilities, clashes of timetables and then you changed the subject.'

Surprise rippled through him. How had she managed to read him so accurately? 'I wanted you here but we're having an affair and I didn't want to put you in a difficult position.'

She raised her brows. 'How is me coming here difficult? People who have affairs can support each other. I want to support you. If I hadn't been able to make it or if I didn't want to come, I would have told you.'

'Yes, I guess you would have.' He looked at her standing there—tall, beautiful with a dazzling aura, yet with an air of concern for him. She'd wanted to come, wanted to be with him tonight in public. His heart sang.

He drew her back into his arms. '*Merci.* It was *miserable* without you.'

'Now, that's what a girl wants to hear.' She laughed, resting her head on his shoulder, her hair brushing his cheek.

His arms tightened around her, the action proprietorial. She was his. He didn't want to share her. He'd missed her so much that evening. He'd gone through the motions of being a host but nothing had sparkled until she'd arrived.

She lit up a room and she lit up his life. He wanted her in his life, in his home, sharing her life with his. Together.

He loved her.

The realisation hit him hard, almost winding him.

In a few short weeks she'd turned his world upside down. She managed to totally infuriate him, drive him crazy, make him laugh, be his lover and his friend. And she'd done all of it at the same time. He wanted to be with her, create a family with her.

Now all he had to do was end this charade of an affair and tell her how he really felt.

CHAPTER NINE

XAVIER'S arms stiffened against her and he stepped back, breaking the contact. She turned as Michael Strachan, Xavier's registrar, stuck his head around the door. 'Charlie, Birth Suite needs you to cover for tea relief as they're a midwife short.'

'Thanks, Michael.' She swallowed her sigh that her break had been cut short and turned back to Xavier. 'Sorry. I'll catch you later, promise.'

He nodded. 'I'll walk over with you.'

'Xavier,' Michael interrupted, his tone serious. 'I need a moment to talk to you about something important.'

She squeezed his arm. 'I'll page you the moment I'm free.' She walked briskly toward Birth Suite.

She pushed open the door to find a heavily pregnant woman sitting upright on the bed, supported by beanbags, her face red with the exertion of pushing.

Kerri, the midwife on duty, wore an anxious expression.

'Everything all right?' Charlie picked up the chart.

'Well, I was going to take a teabreak but now I'm not so sure.' Kerri sounded worried.

Charlie turned toward the patient. 'Hi, Imogen, I'm Charlie Buchanan, a midwife, and I've come to give Kerri a break, but you're sounding to me like you're about to deliver your baby.'

The woman nodded, exhaustion etched in deep lines on her face. 'It's harder than when I had Johnny.'

Charlie laid her hand on the woman's abdomen, feeling the strength of the contraction.

Imogen suddenly leaned forward and pushed again, her perineum swelling as the baby's head came down the birth canal. At the end of the push the baby's head retreated.

'I caught a sight of brown hair.' Charlie gave her an encouraging smile and pulled on some gloves. 'Next push, Imogen, I want you to really bear down and then we'll be delivering your baby.'

'Thank…goodness.' Imogen lay back on the beanbag and Kerri gave her a sip of water and mopped her forehead with a cool cloth.

A minute later Imogen grabbed a lungful of nitrous oxide and pushed. Slowly the baby's head crowned and was delivered.

'Well done, Imogen. With the next contraction the baby will come out.' As the words left her mouth the baby's chin burrowed back into the perineum, looking just like a turtle heading back inside its shell. The turtle sign.

Shoulder dystocia.

The baby's shoulders were stuck in the pelvis. Charlie's heart raced. 'Kerri, page Xavier. *Now!*'

The midwife's face drained of colour as she rushed for the phone.

The mnemonic for the obstetric emergency appeared in her head. HELPERRD. H. She'd sent for help. E. Episiotomy.

She reached for the scissors. 'Sorry, Imogen, but I have to make a small cut here because this baby is being stubborn.'

Somehow she managed to slide the scissors in place and protect the baby's head. *Hurry up, Xavier.*

L. Legs. Imogen needed to have her legs over her head 'Imogen, I'm going to drop the bottom half of the bed and then we need to push your legs over your head.' The lever released with a loud clunk.

The woman looked stunned and scared. 'Why?'

'The baby's shoulders are stuck and this will help to free them.' *I hope.* 'Kerri, help her move her bottom down to this edge then take a foetal heart.' Where the hell was Xavier?

She took in a calm breath, focusing on the task rather than the scared expressions of Imogen and Kerri.

P. Pressure. Apply pressure above the pubic bone to move the anterior shoulder. Charlie placed her hand firmly on Imogen's abdomen. 'Imogen, this is really important. I need you to push as hard as you ever have in your life.'

The door burst open. Xavier and Michael raced in.

'Problem?' Xavier's standard understated question in any emergency echoed around the room.

'Shoulder dystocia. Head delivered one minute ago.' Charlie threw the words out as she applied pressure. She heard the snap of latex as Xavier pulled on gloves.

Relief poured through her.

'Is the baby going to be all right, Doctor?' Imogen's fear-laden voice filled the room.

'That is our intention, Imogen. Your job is to follow every instruction we give you and keep your legs up around your ears. Kerri will help.'

Xavier's glance met Charlie's. 'Apply pressure to the top of the uterus as well as above the pubic bone.'

She nodded in complete understanding.

'Right.' He took a breath. 'Let's deliver this baby.' His

brow furrowed in concentration. 'Deep breath, Imogen.' Somehow with limited room he managed to slowly coax the shoulders around.

Sweat poured off him.

'Two minutes.' Precious time marched on, starkly reminding them that time might win.

The silence in the room bore down on them all. With the baby so low it was almost impossible to find the foetal heart, and with every ticking second the outcome for the baby worsened.

The baby would need resuscitation—it might have a fractured clavicle, even nerve damage to the shoulder. She glanced across the room. Michael had set up the paediatric resuscitation trolley.

'Michael, are you ready for the baby?' Xavier's clipped tone conveyed his anxiety.

'Ready.' Michael spoke quietly.

'Push, Imogen.' Xavier's curt instruction bounced off the walls.

The baby's top shoulder appeared. Xavier murmured in French as he lifted the posterior shoulder and the baby slithered out into his hands.

Thank goodness. But Charlie knew the battle wasn't over yet.

'Imogen, you've had a boy but we need to examine him now.' Xavier nodded to Charlie to take the baby while he delivered the placenta.

She picked the baby up, racing him over to the resuscitation trolley. 'Michael, we need oxygen.'

The limp baby lay under the bright lights, his muscles flaccid, his breathing jerky and his skin tinged blue. Michael stood inert for a moment, staring at the baby.

Charlie grabbed the oxygen mask and bag. 'Michael! Suction. *Now.*' She pushed the laryngoscope into his hand.

'Everything all right over there?' Xavier turned toward them.

'Fine.' Michael picked up the fine-tubed suction catheter and cleared the baby's nose. Then he opened the tiny 'scope and started to aspirate the lungs under the direct vision provided by the laryngoscope.

'Apgar at one minute, four.' Charlie started to rub the baby's arms and legs. 'Come on, mate, breathe properly.'

'How is he?' Imogen's teary voice came from the other side of the room.

Charlie put the stethoscope on the baby's chest. 'More suction.'

Michael re-inserted the tube down the baby's throat.

Charlie prayed only clear mucous would come out. They didn't need meconium-induced pneumonia on top of everything else.

She looked at the clock. The baby was very slow to respond. Michael seemed out of his depth. 'Xavier.'

He immediately came over, responding to the tone of her voice, reading her so well, as only he could. Knowing her and how she thought. Why couldn't he recognise they could have that simpatico outside work?

'What's his heart rate?' His eyes seemed blacker than ever.

'Ninety-five.' Michael's voice wobbled.

'Come on, baby.' Xavier rubbed the infant's sternum gently. He turned to Kerri. 'Call Stuart Mullins.'

'Oh, my God, is he going to be OK?' Imogen's voice cracked on the words.

'We're doing our best. He's just a little slow to start breathing properly.' His accent sounded thicker than usual. It always increased in proportion to his concern.

Charlie continued to bag the baby, the mask dwarfing his small face. *Breathe, please, breathe.*

Slowly, the blue tinge of his skin lightened to a dusky pink and then a bright pink. His chest started to rise and fall.

Michael checked the heart rate. 'One hundred and twenty.' Relief shone in his eyes.

'Excellent, but he needs to go to Special Care Nursery for observation after his mother has had the briefest of brief cuddles.' Xavier carried the baby over to Imogen.

Two minutes later Charlie escorted the baby to Special Care Nursery with Michael. After handing over to the nursery staff, they headed back to the birth suite to debrief.

Xavier had made coffee and handed them both a cup as they walked into the kitchen. 'Michael, tell me, what happened just after the baby was born?'

Discomfort cloaked the registrar. 'I froze. I'm sorry.'

Understanding reflected in Xavier's eyes. 'We all have moments when we freeze. The important thing is working out why. Any ideas?'

Michael slowly stirred his coffee. 'It's to do with what I wanted to talk to you about before the emergency.' He gazed into the hot drink. 'I don't think I'm cut out for obstetrics.'

Shocked surprise rippled through Charlie. 'What do you mean?'

Michael put the spoon down, the action studied and deliberate. He glanced up, looking at both of them. 'Have you ever found yourselves in a job that people encouraged you to do and you suddenly realised it did nothing for you?'

Charlie nodded. 'Oh, yes.' Memories of law came flooding back.

Michael sighed. 'I'm six months away from my final exams in obstetrics. I've spent eight years getting to this point and I don't think I want to be an obstetrician.' The anguish in his voice cut through her.

Xavier's brow furrowed. 'How long have you been feeling like this?'

'Too long. A year at least.'

'That's quite a while.' He shifted his weight against the kitchen bench. 'What are you planning to do about it?'

Michael wrung his hands. 'I wish I knew. I feel like I'm on the edge of a mountain and which ever way I move, I'm going to fall.'

Charlie's mind mulled over what he was saying. 'Have you spoken to Phil about this? I mean, you worked with him for a couple of years so he might be of some help.'

'He reckons I just have pre-exam jitters and that once I've got my qualifications and I'm a consultant, I'll feel differently.'

'I do not agree.' Xavier's deep voice resonated around the room. 'A year is a long time to have been feeling unhappy with what you are doing.'

Charlie spoke from experience. 'Those feelings won't change overnight. If anything, they will intensify.'

Michael nodded, anguish washing across his face. 'I know, but I'm so close to finishing, perhaps I should just sit the damn exams.'

Charlie bit her lip, feeling for Michael as his dilemma washed over her.

Xavier crossed his arms. 'These exams, they are no walk in the park. It is a lot of hard work and energy to pour into something that you are no longer passionate about.'

'But you, Phil, the board, everyone at the hospital has been so good to me I feel I owe it to you all to stay.'

'Ever thought that an obstetrician who is not passionate about what he does isn't doing the best for his patients?'

'Xavier's right,' Charlie chimed in. 'You know how important the patient-doctor relationship is. Women need a care-

giver who is able to meet their emotional needs as well as deliver a baby.' The passion in her voice reminded her of the job she loved.

'So you think I should walk away?' Michael's gaze travelled between the two of them.

She shrugged her shoulders. 'It's not my place to say what you should or shouldn't do. Only you can make that decision.'

'Charlotte's right.' Xavier gave Michael a direct look. 'Only you can make the decision. But you need some help with it, am I right?'

Michael's words came out infused with emotion. 'I feel like I'm suffocating with indecision.'

Xavier dropped a hand lightly onto his shoulder. 'So it's time to focus.'

'What do you want to do now?' Charlie asked softly.

'Last year I volunteered for the Fred Hollows Foundation and spent a month in Vanuatu.' Michael's voice lightened. 'Since then I've wanted to do ophthalmology.'

Xavier spread his hands out in front of him. 'So what's stopping you?'

'You, the hospital, my patients…'

'*Zut.* No, Michael, you are stopping yourself. I am the first to say that if you leave, my workload will double and I might as well just rent a room at the hospital for all that I will see of my home. But that is not important. What is important is that you pursue the path that is right for you, and that you find your passion again.'

Warmth flooded her. Xavier shared her opinion exactly. 'You have to love what you do, Michael. That is what carries you through the day.'

Xavier gave a wry laugh. 'Let's face it, you have thirty-plus years left in your professional life. You must do a job that sets you on fire. Look to the future, to where you want to be, and if it's helping the people of the world see again, then get qualified and get out there and do it.'

Charlie resisted the urge to clap, his eloquent words mirroring her beliefs.

'Thanks, Xavier.' Relief flooded Michael's face and his body relaxed. 'I'll start ringing around tomorrow. I heard Gheringya might have an opening coming up next year.'

'I will give you a reference, Michael. Just let me know.'

'Thanks.' The pager on his belt beeped. 'Excuse me, I'll just take this call.' Michael walked out into the corridor.

Charlie shook her head in amazement. 'That was a brilliant speech you just gave. I've never heard you on your soapbox before.'

'Well, it makes a change, seeing I'm usually listening to you on yours.' His smile softened his words as he reached for her.

'*Touché.* So part of your job is to sort out your staff's life for them?'

'No, Michael's doing that for himself. I just pushed him so he could move from limbo to action. I've known he has not been happy ever since I arrived.'

'That's pretty amazing.'

'What?' For a moment Xavier looked confused.

'To encourage your registrar to leave when he's so close to finishing and when the hospital has invested so much in him.'

'But if he isn't happy, is the hospital really benefiting?'

'I know. But it's still pretty amazing.' Her father's face floated into her mind. If only he'd understood what Xavier seemed to intuit. People had to be true to themselves and follow their calling. She had to be a midwife, and could never have been a lawyer. If her father had seen that, it would have saved a lot of heartache.

'Deep thoughts?' He stroked her face.

She reached up and touched his hand, her fingers tracing the length of his fingers. She sought his gaze and wondered about this gorgeous man who'd come into her life. She hadn't known him very long, but the more time she spent with him, the more she needed to be with him. Needed to be a part of his life, experience his love and care.

To be with this wonderful man who believed people should be true to themselves.

A man who set her blood on fire and filled her waking and sleeping thoughts.

She loved him.

Her breathing stalled. She loved him. She loved this man who would support her dreams.

She wanted a future with him. A family. Their family. Her, Xavier and a baby. Could it be possible?

She dug deep and found her voice. 'Xavier, Jade came to see me the other day. She wants you and I to adopt Ebony.'

Xavier's arms wrapped around her waist. 'She's got good taste. We'd make great parents.'

Her mind raced along with her heart. What was he thinking? Great parents as a separate unit or great parents together? 'Would we?'

'Absolutely. We would make wonderful parents.' He gave her a searching look. 'Is that something you've been thinking about?'

Her heart hammered against her chest. 'I... We're having an affair and...'

'Is that something you've been thinking about?' His voice was low and insistent.

'Yes.' The word came out on a breath.

'Me, too.' He cradled her face in his hands, and gave her a smile full of promise that sent her heart quivering. 'I've been thinking about it for quite a while.'

He lowered his head, capturing her lips, kissing her hard. A kiss of commitment, a kiss of shared dreams.

The shrill of Xavier's phone shattered the moment.

'*Alors.*' Xavier punched the 'on' button. 'Xavier Laurent.'

Charlie watched him take the call, trying to absorb what had just happened.

He snapped his phone shut. 'Heather Birchip is about to deliver.' He picked up Charlie's hand. 'I have to go but we will talk about us soon.'

Charlie nodded and stroked his cheek. 'We will. After you've delivered this baby.'

She watched him leave and hugged the knowledge to herself that he wanted to be with her and raise a family. Her life, which had been like a pile of dust a week before, was rising again like a phoenix. Only this time she had a partner who understood her. She wouldn't be alone again.

CHAPTER TEN

CHARLIE sighed wearily and pushed her arms up over her head, desperately needing to stretch. She sat surrounded by financial spreadsheets, patient histories and the fifty-page document from the maternity coalition. Half-empty cups of cold tea made an arc on her desk and a pile of scrunched-up paper trailed across the floor.

In ten minutes she had the official appointment with Xavier to hear the ruling on the programme. She'd gone over every last detail, memorising all the important statistics.

She couldn't wait to see him. It has been a long two days, their only real contact being stolen kisses as they'd passed in the corridor. Both of them had been flat out with a baby boom brought on by a raging summer storm and a huge drop in barometric pressure. So busy that they hadn't found a quiet hour to have the conversation they needed to have about the future.

Their future.

He saw her as part of his future. Her heart soared again, just as it did every time she thought about it. She'd been walking around with a silly grin on her face and hugging the knowledge close ever since he'd spoken the words, "We will talk about *us* soon."

Today's meeting was the last one for the day so the moment it was squared away they could talk. After that, the evening opened up in front of them. She could hardly wait.

Standing up, she placed the empty cups in the sink, then tucked her notes into the appropriate files. She'd explored every corner of the programme and knew it inside out. Last night she'd had a long phone conversation with Rebecca, the convener of the Perth programme, which was the longest-running community midwifery programme in the country. She'd had some new and convincing arguments.

Any question Xavier asked, she had the facts and figures to give a full and detailed answer. She planned to have the community midwifery programme still functioning at 5.30 p.m.

As she headed out the door with her colour-coordinated folders clutched close to her chest, a bubble of laughter escaped into the air. She'd realized that, just once, she matched Xavier in organisation and neatness.

She pushed open the doors into the administration building and took a deep breath.

'Good afternoon, Charlie.' Dorothy Bailey, Xavier's secretary, gave her a warm smile. 'He won't be long, he's just finishing up talking to the endocrine unit manager.'

'Thanks.' The sooner the meeting started, the sooner she would know the outcome. Adrenaline played havoc with her body. Her heart thumped too quickly, her mouth dried, and it took every ounce of self-control not to drum nervous fingers against the folders on her lap.

Liz, the endocrine unit's nurse manager, walked out of the office smiling, giving Charlie a thumbs-up sign. 'He's extended community nursing for diabetes, which is fantastic. Hope your news is as good as ours. Good luck!'

With trembling legs she stood up and walked to the door. Her fingers curled around the cool metal handle. Pausing for a moment, she breathed in deeply, then pushed open the door.

Xavier stood staring out the window toward the sea. Sunlight played across him, his hair gleaming black with traces of silver streaks.

Familiar heat encircled her and she fisted her hand, forcing away the overwhelming desire to run her hands through his hair.

The door clicked shut behind her.

He turned, his face lined with tiredness, taut with tension. The moment he saw her he smiled.

She melted under the wattage of his smile. She wanted to drop everything and throw her arms around him, feel his body moulded against her own, fitting into her curves as if by design. But she couldn't. This was work. But the moment the meeting was over she would lose herself in his arms for a very long time.

She placed her folders on his desk and sat in the chair, clasping her hands on her lap. 'So here we are.' Her voice sounded strained to her own ears.

'*Oui*, here we are.' He sat down, his gaze riveted to hers, exploring every part of her. 'In some ways it has been a long six weeks, but in others it has been the fastest of my life.'

She nodded, understanding perfectly. Her time with him had been pure magic, surpassing anything she'd ever known. But now wasn't about the two of them—that would come later. 'Xavier, today's been the longest day of my life. I need to know your decision on the community midwifery programme.'

'Yes you do.' He tapped his folder. 'I have been right through this programme, I've seen you at work, I've spoken to the patients. You do a fantastic job with limited resources and clearly the patients adore you. You are a dedicated staff member, an excellent midwife and an asset to this community.'

Charlie scanned his face while she listened to his words. She wanted to glow in his praise but she wouldn't allow herself that luxury. Butterflies pummelled her stomach. What came next?

He pulled out a financial spreadsheet and placed it on top of the pile. 'I have also been through the figures, Charlotte, and at this point, because midwives do not attract a Medicare rebate from the government, the programme is not financially self-supporting.' He took in a breath and caught her gaze. 'I'm very sorry, but the programme has to close.'

Her stomach plummeted. *Please, no.* Blood roared in her ears, and her breath shuddered into her lungs in ragged jerks. 'But I have funding until the end of the financial year.'

He sighed, his regret hanging in the air. 'I know that was the plan but it was also based on the programme paying for itself.' Tiredness clung to him. 'Charlotte, I've been up nights, trying every permutation and combination to make this work for you, for the hospital, but right now the programme is not breaking even.'

Her brain clicked into gear. 'But it could if it had the full twelve months.' She pulled out her projected financial sheet. 'I have increased bookings for the next quarter.'

Xavier nodded, his expression emphatic. 'On paper that looks to be a wonderful thing, but the reality is that with those increased bookings you will need another midwife. Her salary would take the programme back into the red.'

'I wouldn't need another midwife.' Her voice started to rise.

Distress creased his brow. 'Charlotte, you are efficient and competent and a sensational midwife, but you cannot be in two places at once. You are already working long hours. With increased numbers you would need help. You cannot compromise patient safety or your own.'

'In Perth the midwives—'

His hands opened palm upwards, in a familiar gesture of contrition. 'In Perth they are dealing with a larger population than we are in Amaroo. Even the National Maternity Coalition admits that in some rural areas community midwifery programmes are not financially viable without support from another agency. Which is why they are starting to lobby the government for midwife Medicare rebates.'

He ran his left hand through his hair, bringing it along his jaw line, and rested his chin in his palm. 'The bottom line is that as much as I would love this programme to continue, there is no money in the budget to support it. We are barely managing to fund the entire hospital. The Department of Health has given me an ultimatum. I'm sorry, but my hands are tied.'

Her mind grappled with his words. 'But money was allocated to my programme for another quarter. Why cut it now, three months early?'

He bit his lip. 'The money is not there. It comes out of the global budget. Everything has been re-allocated to support viable programmes under direction of the department. In another three months the picture won't have changed. The programme still won't be self-supporting. Stopping it now gives the women time to come to terms with another system.'

Tears pricked the back of her eyes and she blinked furiously. Her project, her baby, which had been so much a part of her, was no longer. She took in a long, trembling breath.

Xavier walked around the desk and knelt down beside her,

quietly handing her an ironed, neatly folded white handkerchief. 'I know this hurts, Charlotte. I understand you've just
lost something very special. I'm really sorry but right now the
hospital cannot afford to run community midwifery. If I could
change things, I would.'

Through tear-filled eyes she saw regret etched on his face.
She couldn't hold herself back from him any longer. Leaning
into him, she dropped her head onto his shoulder, breathing
in his scent of citrus and soap. An overwhelming sense of
coming home streaked through her.

He stroked her back, his calmness permeating her distress.
Six weeks of being on high-alert anxiety to save her programme, drained out of her, exhaustion taking its place. She
wanted to stay on his shoulder for ever, sheltering in his care,
avoid thinking about what happened next. What her working
future held.

'Charlotte,' his voice soothed. 'I know it seems dark right
now and you cannot see the light, but sometimes when we're
forced to take a new road we end up realising the new road
is the one we belong on.'

His words bounced off the haze in her brain. What was he
saying? She raised her head. 'Sorry?'

He cupped his hands around her face. 'I'm talking about
us. Now that the programme has closed, that gives you more
time.'

She dabbed her face with his hankie and cleared her throat.
'I need another job.'

'I know you do. I have the perfect job for you.' He hugged
her. 'Midwife in charge of the antenatal clinic.' He announced
it as if she'd won the lottery.

She moved his hands away from her face. 'You want me
to take on the management of antenatal outpatients?' She

spoke quietly and slowly, trying to understand why he'd even suggest that job.

'You will be wonderful down there.' He smiled, his gaze fixed lovingly on her face.

She stared into his eyes, trying to get a hint of what he was really thinking. 'Well, sure, but I could be great in Birth Suite.'

'But Antenatal needs your skills to modernise it. It's lagging behind other regional hospitals. It also has the added bonus of regular hours, more sociable hours. You have to admit, that would be an improvement.' He smiled encouragingly, as if they were of one mind.

A shiver of unease ran through her. 'Xavier, shift work has never bothered me in the slightest. Yet you want me to take on a nine-to-five administration position because it has more sociable hours. Sociable for who?'

'For us.' He reached for her hand. 'It is the perfect situation. You will still be nursing, doing what you love, and we can concentrate on starting our family. The family we both want so much.'

An arrow of anger pierced her heart, her controlling past rearing its head. 'I don't have to work regular hours to do that.'

His brow furrowed in confusion. 'Right now we both know we have something special but we are never in the same place long enough to fully explore that. Look at the last forty-eight hours. With only one of us working crazy hours, we have more chance of finding time to be together. You'd be doing this for us.'

The small wound in her heart broke open and haemorrhaged. This was her family all over again. Her needs and wants counting for nothing, being completely submerged in other people's desires. Again she was being asked to change to please someone else. Love with soul-destroying conditions, a replica of her mother's life.

It was Richard all over again. Working the job to suit the man. Oh, God, she'd been so stupid to let this happen again.

She took in a deep breath. Surely she must have misunderstood what Xavier really meant. She must have missed something. 'I don't want an administrative position.' *Please, understand. Know that I live to deliver babies.*

'But you are over-qualified to join the nursing bank, which is the only other vacancy at the moment.' He shrugged. 'We don't have to decide right now. I am sure there will be a position somewhere in the hospital that will suit us.'

He pulled her into his arms and nuzzled her neck with his lips. 'Besides, I am hoping there will soon be a wonderful reason for you to stop working altogether.'

His heat surged into her, sending tremors of wondrous sensation through her, her body completely betraying her.

No! Her brain screamed in protest. She pulled away, needing the physical distance between them. *Stop working altogether.* Her blood rushed to her feet. He had no idea who she was, no idea what she needed, what made her Charlie. Hell, he couldn't even call her by her preferred name.

He wanted her to change so she suited him more. *Us.* There was no *us.* He wanted a lover and a mother for his kids, but he wanted a tailor-made package. She'd been down that road before. That wasn't love.

Fighting back tears, she walked to the window, her arms wrapped tightly around her waist, her body and mind crying out in pain. She gazed at a calm, sparkling, blue ocean, twinkling in the summer sunshine. How could it be so calm when her world had just disintegrated? She turned slowly and faced Xavier.

'And what about you? How about I ask you to work regular hours so we can be together?'

An expression of disbelief crossed his face. 'Charlotte, I am obstetrician. We don't have regular hours.'

'Oh, right, and I'm just a midwife so my job is expendable.' Bitterness filled her voice.

'That is *not* what I am saying.' Confusion laced his words. 'I know your work is important to you, which is why I thought this was a perfect solution for us. For us and our family.'

'This isn't a solution, Xavier. This is token effort. Delivering babies is part of who I am. I can't take the job in Antenatal or any other job you dream up for me so it best suits *your* life.'

He moved toward her. 'It's not for me, Charlotte. It's for us. What's best for us.'

Her dreams imploded at his lack of understanding. 'No, Xavier. It's all about you.' She put her arms out in front of her like a barrier, knowing what she had to do. She couldn't let him touch her or she'd crumble. 'You once told me that you needed to look for a partner outside medicine. This is why, isn't it? You want a partner who will live her life around you, making all the compromises. I can't be that person.'

His eyes clouded as he ran his hand through his hair. 'How can you know if you haven't tried?'

Her heart contracted in such pain her breathing stalled. He didn't want her. He wanted a version of her, one that would stifle her until she no longer existed. 'I saw it destroy my mother and it would surely destroy me. Then there'd be no *us*.'

She forced out the words against a tide of tears, hating what she had to say. 'I'm leaving Amaroo. Last night the Perth Community Midwifery convenor offered me a job if mine fell through.'

Pain and disbelief crossed his face. 'How can you leave? How can you just throw away what we have, what we could have, without even trying?'

Because I can't be who you want me to be.

'I want us to be together.' Desperation soaked into his words.

She bit her lip, steeling herself against his grief. Emptiness filled her. 'I'm sorry, it just wouldn't work.'

His shoulders stiffened and a muscle in his jaw spasm. 'So your career is so important to you that you will leave me over a job?'

His words shredded her heart. She forced herself to really look at him, searching for signs of understanding. But there were none. He had no clue, no understanding of where she was coming from.

Where was the man she'd fallen in love with?

All she could see was a man who knew what he wanted, and was used to getting it when he asked. Shades of her father. Love with conditions.

Her legs trembled, the walls threatened to close in on her. She had to leave. There was nothing else left to say. Nothing left to stay for. No understanding could be reached when he had no idea who she was. The fire in her soul spluttered and died, her dreams of a future turned to ashes.

'Goodbye, Xavier.' Somehow she managed to walk to the door and walk through it. She didn't look back.

Xavier swiped the colour-coordinated folders off his desk, their contents spilling out onto the floor with an unsatisfying thud. He slumped into his chair, anger and disbelief whirling inside him.

How could she look at him with those large, emerald eyes

as if he was the one causing the pain? Those eyes in the past few weeks had radiated warmth and affection and two nights ago he'd thought he'd seen something even stronger.

But in a heartbeat she'd walked out the door, throwing away the chance to build on what they had together. Throwing away his love. How could she just leave?

His brain reeled at the events that had just unfolded. He'd known she wouldn't easily accept the loss of the community midwifery programme and he'd agonised over the best way to break the news to her. But his hands were tied. The budget had no fat, no reserves, and as much as he would love to give her the community programme, he couldn't.

Hard decisions had to be made. He'd thought she under-stood that. He'd sown the fiscal seeds of doubt ever since they'd met. He never imagined she would leave him over the decision.   .

Abruptly, he pushed his chair out from the desk and swung it around to the window. The wind had picked up and white-caps now danced on the top of the ocean. He'd missed the moment of change from calm sea to rough. Just like he'd missed the moment Charlotte had changed.

How could she not understand that their relationship was far more important than a job?

Another pile of folders hit the floor. What did the psycholo-gists say about being attracted to the same type of person over and over? He'd let his ragged heart overrule his head. He was an idiot!

He paced across the office. But he knew he wasn't a fool at knowing what made relationships work. He'd watched his parents in action, fostering their relationship, while his relatives' had floundered.

Relationships didn't work if you didn't see each other, if

one person's focus was elsewhere. He wanted to give *this* relationship the perfect conditions to grow.

His anger surged again. Why hadn't she seen the closing door of her programme as being the opening of a new door? A door that could take them to a special place. A place where they could be together and raise a family. It had been so clear to him, almost as if the programme's closing was a gift to them. A gift she'd thrown away, along with his love and his heart.

He looked at the clock. Six p.m. Time to go home.

He hesitated. For the first time in a long time, going home didn't appeal. Too many memories of Charlotte pervaded the house. Her perfume lingered on his sheets, her hairbrush sat in his bathroom and her towel hung by the pool. Almost every room held a memory of the joy she brought him.

Had brought him.

No, he couldn't go home. Not to shattered dreams and the constant reminder of what he'd just lost. He picked up his jacket and his wallet, closed the door on the mess and drove into town.

The band turned the bass up full blast and the walls of the pub vibrated, along with Xavier's head. He pushed the plate of half-eaten food away. On other occasions he'd wolfed down the rump steak grilled to perfection. Tonight it tasted like cardboard.

For three hours he'd sat in the darkest, furthest corner of the pub, nursing a glass of merlot, scowling at anyone who attempted conversation.

Charlotte's face constantly swam in front of his eyes, heightening his pain into a jagged sharpness that intensified with every breath he took. He wished he were on call—at least he could have buried himself in work instead of sitting here like a caricature of a broken lover.

'Hiding out?' Phil Carson put two glasses of beer on the table and slid into the chair opposite him.

'Phil.' Xavier extended his hand, clasping the retired doctor's hand, resigning himself to having to make polite conversation.

'Heard you were here.' Phil sipped his beer.

He raised his brows. 'Village gossip travels quickly.'

'Actually, I haven't heard any gossip, but both Bob Jenkins and David McAllister told me you were sitting here with a look of thunder. They're worried about you.' He leaned back in his chair. 'Bad day?'

'You could say that.' He watched the head on his beer slowly diminish.

Phil stared straight at him. 'Work or personal?'

He wanted to say, *None of your business.* But something in the older man's fatherly expression tugged at him. He sighed. 'Both.'

'Ah, but work wouldn't have brought you to the pub now, would it?'

'You are going to badger me until I tell you, *oui*?'

Phil grinned. 'You got that right.'

Xavier ran the coaster through his fingers. 'I had to cancel Charlotte's community midwifery programme today.'

'How did she take it?'

He grimaced. 'Oh, really well. She is leaving Amaroo and going to work in Perth.'

Phil's air of casualness instantly disappeared. 'Perth? Why Perth?'

'Because the woman is determined to work in community midwifery, and she's putting her job ahead of the people who care for her.' His bitterness spilled into the words.

Phil leaned forward. 'That doesn't sound like Charlie.'

'*Non?* It is a familiar story to me. I've been abandoned for a job before.' He downed the glass of beer, the coolness almost hissing against the heat of his throat.

'Did you ask her to stay?'

Xavier rolled his eyes. 'Of course I asked her to stay. I pleaded with her to stay, but she's determined to go to her dream job.'

Phil rubbed his forehead as if trying to make sense of the conversation. 'Is the job a promotion?'

'I don't know.' Exasperation filled his voice. 'I don't think so. She didn't mention it.'

Phil drew circles in the condensation on the table. 'I've known Charlie for five years, and she loves this town. She loved her community midwifery programme too, but she knew it might fold.' He met Xavier's gaze. 'We've talked about what she might do if the programme ceased and not once did she mention leaving Amaroo. I'm certain she'd happily go back to Birth Suite where she worked before.'

'I offered her a job in Antenatal. A perfect job—Monday to Friday, regular hours, so we could focus on our life together.' Bile scalded his throat. 'She threw it back in my face.'

Phil shot him a look. 'Ah.'

'Ah? *Zut!* What is that supposed to mean?'

Phil crossed his arms. 'Did you ask her what she wanted to do?'

A prickle of unease washed over him. 'I did not ask her to give up work, if that is what you are inferring.' His defensive tone hung in the air. 'I asked her to work nine to five. I thought we had something really special.' He ran his hand through his hair. 'Something we could build on, that would take us into the future where we could grow old together.'

The older doctor placed his hand on Xavier's arm. 'You and I both know that Charlie's only ambition is to care for women and deliver healthy babies.'

Being a midwife is an integral part of who I am. I only ever wanted to deliver babies and I get to do that every day.

His stomach rolled, nausea flooded him. Phil was right—ambition wasn't a force that drove Charlotte. She just wanted to be who she was.

I'm not going to get into a relationship and risk losing 'me' all over again.

In his excitement at the idea of being with her, he'd tried to take from her the *one* thing she needed.

Mon Dieu. He'd asked her to sacrifice her identity. He'd done exactly what her father and fiancé had done. He'd asked her to change to accommodate him and his needs. He'd been patriarchal, judgmental and, oh, so very wrong. Of course she was leaving him.

But not if he could help it. He stood up. 'Phil, I have to go. I have to talk to her.'

The older man smiled. 'Of course you do, son. Drive carefully—there's a storm brewing.'

CHAPTER ELEVEN

CHARLIE tugged her suitcase, pulling it down from the top of her wardrobe, and ducked as a pile of other gear cascaded with it. Spanner leapt out of the way with a yelp.

'Sorry, Span.' She sat on the floor surrounded by the mess, hugging her dog, burying her face in her golden coat. The tears she'd held back for so long rolled down her cheeks, carrying her misery and anguish, merging into a pool of despair.

She'd risked her heart, only to have it returned to her battered, bruised and broken. It hurt so much that she ached inside and out. Everything stretched out in front of her, shattered and bleak.

She'd lost her future—her dreams of sharing a future with Xavier, in the town she loved. And along with it she'd lost her dream of having a family with him. A dream that had come so close to reality she could almost taste it.

And now she was going to Perth.

Spanner licked her face. A few hours ago, in her anger and disbelief, going to Perth had been the perfect solution. She'd have said or done anything to get out of that office. Anything to separate herself from Xavier, who'd had been so unaware of what he'd been asking her to do. What he had asked her to give up.

His insistence that *his* way was the only way, had brought her past flooding back so fast that the emotions had swamped her. She hadn't been able to breathe properly, let alone think.

She half-heartedly opened the case and threw in a few clothes. Why? Why had Xavier been so insistent that she change jobs? The question went around and around in her head, niggling like a thorn in a finger.

Xavier had gone out of his way to create an opportunity for Michael Strachan. He'd encouraged him to take a chance and go with his dreams. He'd behaved in a way so different from her father and Richard that his behaviour this afternoon made no sense. Why would he support Michael in his career and not her?

In a pile of clean laundry she found the pair of overalls Xavier had worn the day Ebony had been born. She hugged the garment close to her and breathed in deeply.

Disappointment rocked her. She'd lost him completely—even his scent had been replaced by that of laundry powder.

Images of the night they'd found Ebony played across her mind. The night they'd agreed to an affair. The night he'd opened up about his past.

The night he'd told her how much he'd been hurt. *Two people couldn't be dedicated to their careers, each other and a family. He was discarded, along with an unborn child.*

Her heart stalled, hope raced in. Did Xavier believe he couldn't be loved if she worked? That she couldn't love their child if she worked? Had he asked her to give up work not because he wanted to change her but because he was scared he would lose her? Scared that she loved her job more than him?

Agitation fizzed in her veins. She had to find out. She needed to talk to him. Needed to know. *Now.*

Riffling through piles of clothes and general mess, she frantically searched for her car keys, finally finding them under her T-shirts. 'Back soon, Span.' She patted the dog and headed to the door.

Spanner started shivering and raced to hide under her bed, howling as she went.

A moment later wind gusted into the house through the open doors, rattling the windows. Charlie peered outside. Black clouds scudded quickly across the sky as jagged bolts of lightning headed earthward. Thunder cracked so loud her heart seemed to bounce off her rib cage.

Huge drops of rain slammed into the house, ricocheting off the tin roof and coming in through the hundred-year-old cracks.

Above the deafening rain and wind she heard the penetrating deepness of a truck's air-horn. Then the sickening sound of crushing metal.

Accident. She dialled 000, giving the operator directions. Grabbing her medical bag and her waterproof coat, she raced out to her car.

Darkness, usually slow to creep in on summer nights, rushed forward with the storm. The car's wheels spun in wet gravel as she headed down the track to the highway. She squinted to see through the windscreen, the wipers working hard against the punishing rain. The short few hundred metres to the main road seemed to extend to ten times their normal length.

She joined the highway and rounded the first bend. A semi-trailer lay across the road, its trailer having jackknifed, taking out two cars on its skidding trajectory.

Her mind raced. *Triage.* Assess the scene. Prioritise. She ran to the crushed car, flattened between the truck and the embankment.

She stopped short, biting her lip. She doubted she could do anything. The occupants had probably died instantly. Rain pelted her. She shone her torch, catching sight of the number plate.

Xavier's car.

Her legs trembled and her body shook uncontrollably. Her stomach heaved. Leaning forward, she vomited into the ditch. She'd lost him. Gone before she could tell him she loved him. Before she could assure him that her job would *never* come ahead of him.

She pulled on a door, frantic to get to him. *You can't be dead. I won't let you be dead.* The door wouldn't move. She cupped her hands around her eyes, trying to see through the tinted window, but all that greeted her was inky darkness. In sheer desperation kicked she door. Nothing moved.

'Xavier!' She heard herself scream, a disembodied voice ragged with pain.

Arms wrapped around her. 'It is all right. I am here.'

She slumped against him, grabbing him with her hands, making sure he was in one piece. Never wanting to let him go. Confusion swam in her shocked mind, her thoughts clawing to hold onto something to make sense of the situation. 'I thought…the car… I thought you…'

He stroked her hair. 'I know. I was coming to see you. I missed the turn-off and hit something, perhaps a wombat. I was out of the car when the truck rounded the corner. I am OK.' He squeezed her tightly against him.

He was coming to see me. The wondrous thought wove through her.

'Charlotte. I need you. I need your help.' His firm 'doctor-in-charge' voice instantly cleared her brain, grounding her, bringing her mind back to the accident.

'The truck driver's dazed and he has a broken arm and lacerations. But I can't get to the woman in the car.' He gripped her arm. 'The heavy-duty tow truck and Jaws of Life are still fifteen minutes away. You might just be small enough to crawl through the space between the car and the truck to reach her.'

Charlie nodded, her training overcoming her shock. 'Do you know who it is?'

'It's Penelope Watson.'

Fear shuddered through her. 'But she's eight months pregnant.'

'*Exactement.* We need to get to her now and assess her and the baby.'

They ran to the car, which was pinned under the back wheels of the truck. The rain continued to pour down, bringing visibility down to zero.

Xavier held the torch. 'I smashed the back window with a rock. See if you can fit between the truck and the car and climb through it. The rain will have washed away any petrol, but be careful. If the fumes are too strong, you come back out.' He gave her a quick hug, his words carrying his concern. 'I mean it, Charlotte, be careful.'

Instinct overrode her terror. She crawled through the gloom. 'Pen.' She yelled to be heard over the rain. Using her hands, she felt for the back of the car as her eyes became accustomed to the gloom.

'Pen, it's Charlie Buchanan.' Glass tore at her legs as she pulled herself through into the car.

Penelope reached out her arms toward her, her eyes wide with shock. 'Charlie?' Her voice quivered with fear.

'Yes, Pen, it's me.' Charlie's fingers closed around the woman's wrist, giving support, checking her pulse. Thready.

'Charlotte.' Xavier's worried voice sliced through the dark. 'Are you all right?'

'I'm with her. I'm checking her vital signs.'

Penelope's seat belt held her in her seat. Although she looked unhurt, her rapid pulse told a different story. 'Pen, do you have any pain?'

'I've got a tight feeling down here.' She put her hand on the lap sash of the belt that crossed her abdomen.

Charlie undid the seat belt and gently pressed her hand against Penelope's abdomen. Rigid. Internal bleeding.

A shiver of dread cut through her. The impact of the accident would have been enough to cause a placental tear or a rupture in the uterus. Both mother and baby could die.

Panic rose. She forced it down. 'Xavier, I need more light.'

'I am working on it.' His voice reassured her. Help was on its way.

Maintain circulating volume. 'I need to put in an IV, Pen, to help you and the baby.'

Penelope's hands flew to her abdomen, flattening out under the baby in a cradling action. 'Charlie, the baby…I'm not going to lose my baby, am I?'

Penelope's fear ripped into her. Pen needed to be in an operating theatre right this minute, with Xavier weaving his life-saving magic. Instead, she was trapped in a car, in the middle of a rainstorm, with a midwife with limited equipment.

Where the hell was the ambulance?

Where the hell was the light she needed? She couldn't insert an IV by feel alone.

Stabilise her. The tourniquet snapped into place. Her

fingers probed for a vein. Nothing. Penelope's shocked veins had collapsed. 'Let's try the other arm, Pen.' *Please.*

Bright light flooded the interior of the car. *Thank you, SES.*

She could feel and see a vein. 'This might sting a bit, Pen.' The cannula slid in. She held her breath. Blood entered the needle. *Yes.* She opened the drip full bore, pushing normal saline into her patient, attempting to replace the fluid she suspected was pouring into Penelope's abdomen.

'Pen, I'm sorry but I need to feel if you've lost any blood. I need to put my hand between your legs.'

The other woman looked vacantly at her, all her thoughts centred on her baby.

Charlie's hands met dampness—warm, congealed blood. The life force of the mother. And the unborn child. Penelope needed a Caesarean section. Now.

'Charlotte, is she stable?' The concern and caring in Xavier's voice swam around her, giving her strength.

'We need to get her out now. She's bleeding.'

She heard his muffled expletive. 'We're doing everything we can at this end. Keep pumping in the saline. The moment the ambulance arrives I'll pass in the plasma expander. *Chérie*, you're doing great.'

Great wasn't enough. It was impossible to do a foetal heart so she had no idea of the baby's condition. Part of her didn't want to know.

Hope was all they had.

She checked Pen's blood pressure. 'Xavier, BP is holding.' *Just.*

'Good. The rescue tow truck's arrived. We're going to jack the trailer off the car. You'll be out soon.' Xavier's voice sounded forced, overly bright.

Be quick. I can't hold her for too long. Charlie infused lightness into her voice. 'Did you hear that, Pen? We'll have you in hospital soon.'

She held Pen's hand but the woman didn't flinch. She was directing all her energy to her unborn child, willing her baby to live.

The nauseating sound of crushing metal boomed in her ears, sending shivers through her. Anxiety, fear and anticipation built on top of each other, making Charlie's heart pound hard and fast.

Then there were arms touching Charlie, voices surrounding her. And Xavier. She didn't want to let Xavier out of her sight. The memory of thinking she'd lost him for ever stayed sharp and strong.

He quickly squeezed her shoulder. Then he and James Rennison lifted Pen onto the stretcher and loaded her into the ambulance. Charlie climbed in after them, securing the door.

The brief moment of relief she'd experienced when Pen had been removed from the car had fizzled out. Nothing had changed. Pen was desperately ill. The high-pitched siren pierced the night, the ambulance speeding against time to get Penelope to Theatre before she and the baby died.

They raced through A & E straight up to Theatre.

'Xavier, I want to scrub in.' She needed to be in Theatre with Pen. With Xavier. She didn't want to be apart from either of them.

His raven eyes filled with emotion. 'I want you in there, too.' He turned and called across the scrub area. 'Phillip, we need her anaesthetised in record time. Charlotte's kept them going this long but neither is going to hold on much longer.'

He scrubbed up and entered theatre. 'How's she going?'

'She's intubated and ready.' Phillip checked the ECG.

'Right, let's get started.' Xavier picked up the scalpel, deftly made an incision, quickly located the uterus and delivered a purply-blue, extremely distressed baby.

Stuart Mullins raced the meconium-stained, limp baby over to the resuscitation cart.

'*Zut*. I can't see a thing here. More suction!' Xavier's curt command radiated his fear that Penelope might die on the table.

Charlie kept the suction in place, keeping the field as clear as possible. Blood bubbled up as fast as she could remove it, quickly building up in the suction bottle at their feet.

Beads of sweat lined Xavier's brow. No matter what he tried, the uterus wouldn't contract. The bleeding continued.

'Xavier, we're risking disseminated intravascular coagulation with this amount of blood loss.' The concern in Phillip's voice rang around Theatre. 'Urine output down.'

'What do you want to do?' Charlie asked the question—the code for a hysterectomy.

Xavier's body vibrated with frustration. 'Give her more Synto. I want to save this uterus.'

'Pressure's dropping.' Phillip spoke over the incessant warning beeps of the BP machine. 'No more time, mate.'

'Clamp—now!'

Charlie ignored the anger in Xavier's voice. She knew he hated that he had to take away Pen's opportunity to have another child.

The ECG machine screamed as the green display morphed into a flat line. 'Cardiac arrest. Start compressions.'

Charlie pressed down on Pen's sternum, each compression a frantic desire to save a life.

Xavier's brow creased in deep furrows as he applied clamps.

Time stood still.

'Come on, Pen.' Xavier's voice sounded low and urgent behind his mask.

Phillip shocked Pen's heart, urging it to restart.

'The uterine artery is now tied off.' Xavier gave Charlie a look of pure relief.

The cardiac monitor's scream segued into regular beeps. 'Sinus rhythm, thank goodness.' Phillip's head appeared over the drape. 'I don't want to go through that again any time soon. It's always harder when it's someone you know well.'

Charlie nodded, too emotional to speak. It had been far too close to tragedy.

'Baby's doing well.' Stuart Mullins pushed past with the isolette. 'I'm taking her down to Special Care now.'

Thirty minutes later Penelope left Theatre, transferred to Intensive care. Xavier tore off his gloves, the latex ripping with the force. He tossed them into the bin. His foot released the bin pedal and the lid crashed closed.

'Alors.' He ran his hand through his hair, the action jerky.

'You saved the baby.' Charlie walked over to him, putting her hand on his shoulder, wanting to comfort him. 'You saved the mother. Focus on that.'

He turned to face her. 'Penelope's not out of the woods yet. The next twenty-four hours are vital. DIC…'

'She'll make it.' She smiled, trying to take away the bleak look in his eyes.

Xavier put his hand over hers. 'You were fantastic out there tonight. Gutsy and brave. *Merci.*'

'I was scared stiff, but you being there helped.' She wanted to drop her head on his shoulder, take refuge in his arms, but first they needed to talk. Solve this impasse between them.

As if reading her mind, Xavier stepped back from her and

undid his gown. 'Two hours ago I was on my way to talk to you. I still need to do that.' He undid the top tie of her gown, his fingers brushing the back of her neck.

Shivers of longing passed through her. She pulled her gown off, dumping it into the linen skip, and then walked over to the now bare operating table. She sat down, swinging her legs, deliberately putting some distance between them.

'Two hours ago I was about to come into town to talk to you.' She stared straight at him, wanting to see his reaction to the question she was about to ask. 'I need to know the real reason you want to push me into a desk job.'

Contrition washed over his face. 'Because I was stupid and insensitive and desperately scared. Scared of you leaving me. *Je suis désolé*, Charlotte. I am so very sorry.'

His contrition and angst washed over her and she longed to comfort him. *Wait and listen*, her rational voice cautioned her. *Let him explain.* 'Why would you think I would leave you?'

He sat down next to her. 'For too long I have been blaming the wrong thing for my failed relationships. I thought work had been the problem. But I now realise that the job had no impact on the relationship at all. All this time I've been blaming the wrong thing. It was not the job or career that was the problem. It was a lack of love.'

She nodded in understanding, a shoot of hope opening up inside her.

He reached for her hand. 'I thought if your focus was so much on your job, you couldn't work and love me.' He shook his head. 'All I ended up doing was behaving like your father, asking you to change and pushing you away.'

He raised her hand to his lips. 'I don't want you to change. I don't want to push you away. I want you to stay.'

His words carried his sorrow into her heart. She wanted to throw her arms around him but nothing was solved. Yet. 'I want to stay too, but how do you see that happening?'

His earnest look entreated and she knew he'd gone through agonies since she'd last seen him. 'You understand I can't offer you what you had for all the reasons I outlined yesterday. But we both know you love a challenge and so, with that in mind, I can offer you something else.'

Her heart turned over. She closed her eyes and breathed in deeply. She had to focus, keep on track. There was too much at stake. 'What is it?'

'Two days ago I got an email from the Health Department. There is ongoing funding for work with teenage girls. If you stay, you will be setting up and running a clinic-cum-health education programme to reduce the number of teenage pregnancies. Also, you'd be supporting kids like Jade when they are pregnant, being their midwife and hospital liaison, delivering their baby and following up well into the postnatal period.'

Charlie's mind tilted on its axis. Xavier was offering her a job. Not just any job. A huge job, one as big as community midwifery. Almost more important in terms of health impact.

Her eyes searched his face. 'You realise the time commitment this programme will take as I set it up?'

He nodded. 'It will be enormous, but if it means you'll be in Amaroo, that is all that matters.'

She blinked back a rush of happy tears. 'What made you change your mind?'

'You once said to me that two careers could be combined if both people wanted it to work. I really want it to work. I love you and I don't want to live without you.'

He really loves you. Her heart soared with wonder. He'd accepted who she was and recognised what was important to her. He'd changed his plans and compromised so he could be with her.

She reached out, laying her palm against his cheek, soaking in the love that radiated from his eyes. She looked deeply into those black eyes full of love. 'Tonight I thought you were dead and all I could think was I hadn't told you how much I loved you. How you've opened my eyes and showed me that living alone is not the way I want to live. No job I ever have will come before you.'

He smiled. 'I know that.'

'And you know that no job will come ahead of our children either.'

'*Oui.* I do.' He slipped off the table and stood in front of her. 'Charlotte, will you accept the job, and accept me too, by marrying me?'

She reached for him, drawing him in close. 'Is it a two-deal package?'

'Only if you want it to be.' The sincerity in his voice pierced her heart.

'I do.' She slid off the table into his arms. 'I do have a condition, though.'

'What is it?' The resignation in his voice played around them.

She ran her hands through his hair. 'No need to panic. I think you'll be OK with this and it won't cost too much of the hospital's money.'

He raised his brows. 'Why do I get the feeling I should be worried?'

She put her finger against his lips. 'I'll set up and run the programme as long as I can train another midwife to take over when I'm on maternity leave.'

He pulled her tightly against him, burying his face in her hair. 'I think that is a wonderful idea.'

'And you need to find ongoing money for that midwife because she'll be an integral part of the programme. Once we're parents, I'll only be working part time.'

Xavier tilted her head, staring deep into her eyes. 'I love you. From the moment I met you, you've changed my world, and made every day a glorious adventure.'

Happiness cascaded through her. 'I love you, too.'

His lips came down to meet hers, two people merging into one, accepting each other, evolving together.

Xavier reluctantly drew away. 'Let's get out of here. Let's go home.'

Charlie tilted her head to the side. 'And where is home?'

He rolled his eyes. 'Your hairbrush is in my bathroom and I have neatly folded towels and a fluffy bathrobe waiting for you.'

She gave him a grin. 'I have a pile of dirty washing on my bathroom floor.'

'Now, why doesn't that surprise me?' He swung her back into his arms. 'I've just thought of a condition of my own.'

'Really?'

'Really. We're increasing Mrs McDonald's cleaning and tidying hours.'

Charlie laughed. 'I can live with that as long as I'm with you.'

'You, me and Amaroo. Now I've got everything I've ever wanted.'

'So have I.' She leaned up, capturing his lips with hers in a brief, tantalising kiss. 'Take me home, Xavier. Take me to *our* home.'

He grabbed her hand, flicked off the lights and together they walked toward their future.

EPILOGUE

XAVIER swung two-year-old Amélie up onto his shoulders and held Luc's hand as they walked home from the park. The sensation of a warm little hand in his larger one always sparked a sense of overwhelming joy.

As they walked they stopped and chatted to friends and peered into prams to see how the babies that he had delivered were growing.

'Papa, I love Wednesday afternoons.'

He glanced down at his four-year-old son. 'Why is that?'

'Because we feed the ducks. Then we go home and you cook dinner. And Mummy always comes home at dinnertime with a big smile. Then she sits down, hugs us and says, "I love Wednesdays."'

Xavier smiled. 'I love Wednesdays, too.' He fished a key out of his pocket but the back door opened unexpectedly.

'Mummy!' Amélie stretched her arms out, almost toppling off Xavier's shoulders.

Charlotte reached out with a wide smile, steadying her. 'Anyone would think I'd been gone for days instead of a few hours.'

Xavier lifted his daughter from his shoulders then leaned

forward to kiss his wife. 'Luc and I have just been discussing Wednesdays.'

She walked inside with him, her arm around his waist. 'I know you love Wednesdays.'

He pulled her into his arms. 'And you do, too. You get to go out into my world and I get to come home into yours.'

'True, I love Wednesdays.' She smiled at him. 'How would you feel if in a few months' time I gatecrashed your Wednesdays for a while?'

He stepped back, looking into dancing, emerald eyes, trying to read her. Five years of married life and she still amazed him, lighting up his world, giving him so much pleasure. He grinned. 'As long as I still get to cook.'

She swatted his arm in a mock huff. 'Luc tells me my cookies are wonderful.'

'*Oui*, but he has French blood and knows how to charm.' He laughed at the indignation on her face. He tucked a few stray strands of hair behind her ear. '*Chérie*, tell me why do you want to share our Wednesdays?'

'Actually, it won't just be me.' She threw her arms around his neck. 'The Laurent family is increasing by one next spring.'

Delight ricocheted through him, expanding the happiness his life already offered him every day. '*C'est magnifique*, my darling.' He wrapped his arms around her, holding her against his heart, giving thanks for his blessings.

Small arms hugged his legs and waist. 'Family hug, family hug.'

His laughter merged with Charlotte's as they opened their arms to their children, hugging them close. His family.

Everything he ever wanted was right here with him in this room. He sighed in contentment. Life didn't get any better than this.

0407 Gen Std HB

MAY 2007 HARDBACK TITLES

ROMANCE™

Bought: The Greek's Bride *Lucy Monroe*	978 0 263 19620 7
The Spaniard's Blackmailed Bride *Trish Morey*	
	978 0 263 19621 4
Claiming His Pregnant Wife *Kim Lawrence*	978 0 263 19622 1
Contracted: A Wife for the Bedroom *Carol Marinelli*	
	978 0 263 19623 8
Willingly Bedded, Forcibly Wedded *Melanie Milburne*	
	978 0 263 19624 5
Count Giovanni's Virgin *Christina Hollis*	978 0 263 19625 2
The Millionaire Boss's Baby *Maggie Cox*	978 0 263 19626 9
The Italian's Defiant Mistress *India Grey*	978 0 263 19627 6
The Forbidden Brother *Barbara McMahon*	978 0 263 19628 3
The Lazaridis Marriage *Rebecca Winters*	978 0 263 19629 0
Bride of the Emerald Isle *Trish Wylie*	978 0 263 19630 6
Her Outback Knight *Melissa James*	978 0 263 19631 3
The Cowboy's Secret Son *Judy Christenberry*	978 0 263 19632 0
Best Friend...Future Wife *Claire Baxter*	978 0 263 19633 7
A Father for Her Son *Rebecca Lang*	978 0 263 19634 4
The Surgeon's Marriage Proposal *Molly Evans*	978 0 263 19635 1

HISTORICAL ROMANCE™

Dishonour and Desire *Juliet Landon*	978 0 263 19760 0
An Unladylike Offer *Christine Merrill*	978 0 263 19761 7
The Roman's Virgin Mistress *Michelle Styles*	978 0 263 19762 4

MEDICAL ROMANCE™

Single Dad, Outback Wife *Amy Andrews*	978 0 263 19800 3
A Wedding in the Village *Abigail Gordon*	978 0 263 19801 0
In His Angel's Arms *Lynne Marshall*	978 0 263 19802 7
The French Doctor's Midwife Bride *Fiona Lowe*	
	978 0 263 19803 4

MILLS & BOON®

0407 Gen Std LP

MAY 2007 LARGE PRINT TITLES

ROMANCE™

The Italian's Future Bride *Michelle Reid*	978 0 263 19447 0
Pleasured in the Billionaire's Bed *Miranda Lee*	
	978 0 263 19448 7
Blackmailed by Diamonds, Bound by Marriage *Sarah Morgan*	
	978 0 263 19449 4
The Greek Boss's Bride *Chantelle Shaw*	978 0 263 19450 0
Outback Man Seeks Wife *Margaret Way*	978 0 263 19451 7
The Nanny and the Sheikh *Barbara McMahon*	978 0 263 19452 4
The Businessman's Bride *Jackie Braun*	978 0 263 19453 1
Meant-To-Be Mother *Ally Blake*	978 0 263 19454 8

HISTORICAL ROMANCE™

Not Quite a Lady *Louise Allen*	978 0 263 19391 6
The Defiant Debutante *Helen Dickson*	978 0 263 19392 3
A Noble Captive *Michelle Styles*	978 0 263 19393 0

MEDICAL ROMANCE™

The Christmas Marriage Rescue *Sarah Morgan*	978 0 263 19347 3
Their Christmas Dream Come True *Kate Hardy*	
	978 0 263 19348 0
A Mother in the Making *Emily Forbes*	978 0 263 19349 7
The Doctor's Christmas Proposal *Laura Iding*	978 0 263 19350 3
Her Miracle Baby *Fiona Lowe*	978 0 263 19539 2
The Doctor's Longed-for Bride *Judy Campbell*	978 0 263 19540 8

JUNE 2007 HARDBACK TITLES

ROMANCE™

Taken: the Spaniard's Virgin *Lucy Monroe*	978 0 263 19636 8
The Petrakos Bride *Lynne Graham*	978 0 263 19637 5
The Brazilian Boss's Innocent Mistress *Sarah Morgan*	
	978 0 263 19638 2
For the Sheikh's Pleasure *Annie West*	978 0 263 19639 9
The Greek Prince's Chosen Wife *Sandra Marton*	
	978 0 263 19640 5
Bedded at His Convenience *Margaret Mayo*	978 0 263 19641 2
The Billionaire's Marriage Bargain *Carole Mortimer*	
	978 0 263 19642 9
The Greek Billionaire's Baby Revenge *Jennie Lucas*	
	978 0 263 19643 6
The Italian's Wife by Sunset *Lucy Gordon*	978 0 263 19644 3
Reunited: Marriage in a Million *Liz Fielding*	978 0 263 19645 0
His Miracle Bride *Marion Lennox*	978 0 263 19646 7
Break Up to Make Up *Fiona Harper*	978 0 263 19647 4
Marrying Her Billionaire Boss *Myrna Mackenzie*	
	978 0 263 19648 1
Baby Twins: Parents Needed *Teresa Carpenter*	978 0 263 19649 8
The Italian GP's Bride *Kate Hardy*	978 0 263 19650 4
The Doctor's Pregnancy Secret *Leah Martyn*	978 0 263 19651 1

HISTORICAL ROMANCE™

No Place For a Lady *Louise Allen*	978 0 263 19763 1
Bride of the Solway *Joanna Maitland*	978 0 263 19764 8
Marianne and the Marquis *Anne Herries*	978 0 263 19765 5

MEDICAL ROMANCE™

The Consultant's Italian Knight *Maggie Kingsley*	
	978 0 263 19804 1
Her Man of Honour *Melanie Milburne*	978 0 263 19805 8
One Special Night... *Margaret McDonagh*	978 0 263 19806 5
Bride for a Single Dad *Laura Iding*	978 0 263 19807 2

MILLS & BOON®   0507 Gen Std LP

JUNE 2007 LARGE PRINT TITLES

ROMANCE™

Taken by the Sheikh *Penny Jordan*	978 0 263 19455 5
The Greek's Virgin *Trish Morey*	978 0 263 19456 2
The Forced Bride *Sara Craven*	978 0 263 19457 9
Bedded and Wedded for Revenge *Melanie Milburne*	
	978 0 263 19458 6
Rancher and Protector *Judy Christenberry*	978 0 263 19459 3
The Valentine Bride *Liz Fielding*	978 0 263 19460 9
One Summer in Italy... *Lucy Gordon*	978 0 263 19461 6
Crowned: An Ordinary Girl *Natasha Oakley*	978 0 263 19462 3

HISTORICAL ROMANCE™

The Wanton Bride *Mary Brendan*	978 0 263 19394 7
A Scandalous Mistress *Juliet Landon*	978 0 263 19395 4
A Wealthy Widow *Anne Herries*	978 0 263 19396 1

MEDICAL ROMANCE™

The Midwife's Christmas Miracle *Sarah Morgan*	978 0 263 19351 0
One Night To Wed *Alison Roberts*	978 0 263 19352 7
A Very Special Proposal *Josie Metcalfe*	978 0 263 19353 4
The Surgeon's Meant-To-Be Bride *Amy Andrews*	
	978 0 263 19354 1
A Father By Christmas *Meredith Webber*	978 0 263 19551 4
A Mother for His Baby *Leah Martyn*	978 0 263 19552 1